The Billionaire's

Best Friend

THE SHERBROOKES OF NEWPORT

BOOK ONE

CHRISTINA TETREAULT

The Billionaire's Best Friend
© 2013, Christina Tetreault

For more information on the author and her works, please see www.christinatetreault.com

The author would like to give a special thank you to the following people:
Angelique Miller and Becka Lynn for letting me "borrow" their dogs JoJo and Maggie.
Dr. Bryan K. Harrell, LT Medical Corp U.S. Navy for answering my questions regarding the military.

Prologue

No one will notice if I sneak outside for a minute. Tugging at the cuff of her sweater, Lauren McDonald crossed the room to the French doors leading outside. A cold blast of air hit her head-on, a stark contrast to the warmer temperature inside the apartment, but it didn't deter her.

Outside, she took a deep breath and exhaled as she took in the view of the city. From the balcony she caught sight of the Prudential Building, or the Pru as Bostonians called it, lit up with the official logo of the New England Patriots, who were at that moment winning the Super Bowl by two touchdowns.

I can breathe again. The thought made no sense

because the penthouse apartment consisted of more square footage than her own home, but thanks to Shelia Wentworth's overpowering perfume, she'd felt starved of air. Lauren looked back inside at the party's other guests. She caught a glimpse of Mark Wentworth, the governor's son, and Henry Fuller, some bigwig defense attorney and owner of the downtown Boston apartment.

When Kevin had invited her to the Super Bowl party, she'd realized it would be different from the ones she'd attended in the past. Considering the people Kevin called friends, how could it be anything else? And she'd been correct. This party didn't have any plastic bowls filled with chips and salsa. There were no buffalo wings and pepperoni pizza from Tim's Pizza. Her nephew didn't keep popping into the room hoping to stay up past his bedtime and watch the game like he had the year before. Oh no, none of that for this refined crowd.

Instead, a professional wait staff served clams casino and sushi. A trained bartender mixed drinks, while fine champagne was chilled in the event the Patriots won tonight. The entire evening felt more like a wedding reception than a football party with friends.

In many ways the party tonight was more like the fundraisers and other social events she attended, thanks to her friendship with Callie Talbot. The only real difference between those events and this one was she had Callie and her family around at those times. Both the Talbots and the Sherbrookes made an effort to make her feel welcome.

With the exception of Kevin Walsh, her date, she couldn't say the same about the people here tonight. While the other guests were cordial, they made little effort to include her in their discussions which revolved around topics she couldn't relate to. The two women she'd been standing with had launched into a comparison of their favorite haunts in Monaco. While Callie and her family might also have favorite spots in the tiny country so popular among the wealthy, they'd find a topic that mattered to them all, including her.

Kevin was like that, too. Since their first date, he'd gone out of his way to find things they had in common. Surprisingly, they had a lot of the same interests. They liked the same music, had similar tastes in movies, and both enjoyed the theater.

Somehow, though, the behavior of the other guests didn't bother her tonight. Although the reaction had dissipated somewhat over the past two years, usually her insides still got all tied up at events like this one. She'd become painfully aware that she didn't belong. Tonight, however, that was not the case. With the exception of the nausea caused by Sheila's perfume, she felt relaxed, if not somewhat bored with the other women's conversation.

A fat snowflake landed on her arm, and Lauren glanced up. Earlier in the evening the sky had sparkled with stars and a large full moon. Now only a few stars remained visible among the clouds. The meteorologist had called for a forty percent chance of snow tonight, and it appeared as though he'd been correct. Even with the snowflakes drifting down, Lauren remained outside, enjoying a few more minutes away from the world inside the apartment.

"There you are. I've been looking for you." Kevin's hand settled on her waist and pulled her close. "What are you doing out here? Are you okay?"

She heard the concern in his voice. The polite thing would've been to find him before she went outside. "I'm fine. Just wanted some fresh air and a chance to check out the view before the game starts again. The city looks beautiful from up here. We can go back in if you want." Lauren moved so she faced him, and once again the thought that he belonged on a movie set rather than inside a corporate office struck her. She'd had the very same thought the evening he'd first approached her.

She'd accompanied Callie to a fundraiser in New York several weeks earlier. When she'd walked into the Waldorf Astoria, the last thing on her mind was a boyfriend. It'd been eleven months since her last relationship ended, and in that time she hadn't been on a single date. Yet, when Kevin approached her she hadn't shied away. In fact, when she saw Callie start back for their table, she'd thrown her a *don't come back just yet* look. From that point on, they had talked all night. Then before she left, he'd asked for her number. When she'd given it to him, she'd half expected him not to call. After all, unlike the guests in attendance, she didn't have millions sitting in her bank account, and he knew that. During their lengthy conversation, she'd told him she taught elementary school. Regardless, the following evening he called, and the next weekend they went out.

"Let's stay out here for a few more minutes. The half-time show just ended." He cut off any rebuttal with a kiss.

The warmth from his body seeped into hers, chasing away her goosebumps. Lauren threw herself into the kiss. She could taste the alcohol on his breath. It had to be a cocktail from the bar. She'd never seen Kevin touch a beer. Instead, he always ordered Manhattans and Old Fashions, drinks that seemed better suited to men from her father's generation.

Kevin pulled his lips away. "I'm glad you came tonight. Are you enjoying yourself?"

"Yes, very much."

"Do you have plans next Saturday?" Kevin leaned back against the railing, his hand locked around hers. "*Hamlet* opens at the Wang Theater."

"Sounds nice."

Behind them the French doors opened. "The game is back on," Mark Wentworth called out to them.

"I think that's our cue."

"Only if you're ready." Kevin rubbed his thumb over her knuckles. "We can stay out here for a few more minutes."

She appreciated the sentiment, but it made no sense for them to stay outside. "I've had enough fresh air."

Kevin kept Lauren tucked up against him as they joined the others. She'd claimed the view and fresh air had pulled her outside, and he hoped that was the only reason she'd left the party. When he'd left her alone with Mark's and Henry's wives, he'd assumed she would be at ease with the women. After all, she possessed an outgoing personality and regularly spent time with the likes of Callie Talbot and Sara Sherbrooke. He wanted Lauren to enjoy herself—get to know his friends and business associates.

"Are you hungry?" Kevin asked as he led her toward an empty love seat. On the large screen television, the Patriots' offense was preparing for the first play of the second half.

Lauren shook her head and took a seat on the edge of the cushion. "All set."

Sitting down next her, he pulled her back to him. "If you change your mind, let me know." He took hold of her hand and let most of his attention return to the game.

Chapter 1

Lauren read the final paragraph of the essay and laughed. Her students never ceased to amaze her. As a way to combine language arts with their current science unit on space she'd asked them to write an essay about what they thought life on the moon would be like. She'd known some of her students had fantastic imaginations, but each of her fifth-graders amazed her with this assignment. The essays not only demonstrated their knowledge of the moon, but also showcased how far their writing skills had progressed since the start of the school year.

After writing a short note at the bottom of the most recent paper, Lauren put a grade in the top right-hand corner and added it to the corrected pile before recording the grade in her computer. She was about to reach for another essay when the doorbell echoed through her tiny ranch house, followed by JoJo's barking. Taking a quick peek out the window, she recognized the dark green Mercedes parked in her driveway. *Right on time as always.* Lauren moved away from the window and toward the front door.

"Happy birthday." Callie Talbot, her best friend since high school, stepped forward and gave Lauren a hug as soon as she opened the door, despite the large bag hanging from one arm and the large box in her hand.

"Thank you. Come on in," Lauren said, returning the hug. "How was the drive?" Closing the door, she followed her friend, who was more like a sister, into the living room.

"Not bad. I stopped to see Helen on the way here."

Lauren joined Callie on the couch. "How is she?" Helen Lee had been Callie's mom's best friend, and since her mom's death a couple of years earlier, Callie went out of her way to stay in contact with the woman.

"Good. Her third grandchild was born last month. She had a ton of pictures to show me. And she said to say hello." Callie set the bag down on the coffee table. "I can get my overnight bag from the car later, but I wanted to give you this now." Reaching into the bag, Callie pulled out a small box wrapped with a pink bow, as well as a large cake box. "I saw these and thought of you." She handed Lauren the small box.

Unwrapping the small box, Lauren smiled when

she pulled open the lid. Nestled inside were long pink earrings in the shape of ballet slippers. The pair would fit in perfectly with her school jewelry. Every day she wore a different pair of silly earrings. She'd started doing it as a student teacher eleven years ago, and somehow it had become her thing. Now all her students expected it, and many gave her earrings as end-of-year gifts.

"They're perfect. Thank you."

"That's not all I have. I brought a red velvet cake from Rosie's bakery, and this is also for you." Callie handed her the larger box she'd been holding.

"Red velvet from Rosie's. That will be gone tonight." Lauren eyed the bakery box as she accepted the other gift her friend held out. Unlike the first gift, which had been wrapped in paper decorated with balloons, this one was wrapped in silver paper and an intricately tied bow adorned the top. Callie hadn't wrapped this box. The only time she put a bow on a box was when it had a self-adhesive back attached to it.

"You didn't need to get me anything." Lauren played with the bow, not wanting to disturb the beautifully wrapped gift.

Callie shrugged. "I know, but I wanted to. Now open it. I've been dying to give this to you since I bought it last week."

Lauren rolled her eyes. "You've gotten bossy since getting married, chickie. You know that, don't you? More impatient, too. I think your husband is rubbing off on you." Slowly, just to annoy her friend,

Lauren untied the bow and carefully tore off the paper. "How is he?" Lauren folded the paper after she unwrapped the present.

Callie grabbed the paper from her hands and balled it up then tossed it on the end table. "He's great. Now will you open it already before I do it for you?"

Lauren pulled open the box and her jaw dropped. Inside the box was perhaps the most gorgeous gown she'd ever seen. Just looking at it she knew it wasn't something you could pick up at the nearby mall.

"I saw it in Saks and thought of you." For the most part, Callie hadn't changed her style or shopping preferences despite her change in financial status. Yet every once in a while she popped into stores like Saks and Gucci. "You need to open the envelope, too." She elbowed Lauren in the side when Lauren didn't move.

So overwhelmed by the gown, she'd missed the envelope sitting on top of it. Gingerly, she picked it up and pulled out two tickets to the ballet *Giselle* being performed in New York City and a printout for hotel reservations at a nearby Sherbrooke Hotel.

"I thought you'd like a new gown for the show. I knew you liked the gown I wore to the New Year's Eve party. This one reminded me of it when I saw it on display."

For a moment Lauren couldn't speak around the lump in her throat. She loved that ballet and had always wanted to see it performed in New York City, but she had considered the endeavor too expensive. Instead she opted for local shows. At one time, Callie would've thought the same way. This extravagant gift only reminded her of how different their lives had become. Lauren looked down at the gown again, a twinge of sadness dampening the happiness she'd felt when Callie had arrived. Sometimes it would be nice to turn back time for a day or two. Make things the way they'd been before Callie had learned her father was Warren Sherbrooke and she'd married billionaire Dylan Talbot.

"I . . . you, shouldn't have. I can't accept all this. It's too much."

Callie waved a hand in her direction dismissing her comment. "I thought you and Kevin could go."

After sticking the tickets back in the envelope, Lauren reached over and gave Callie a hug. "Thank you. If he can't go, I'll ask Kelly or maybe my mom. Kelly may not be up for it. She looks like she might pop any day now," Lauren said, referring to her older sister. "I'd ask you, but I know how you feel about the ballet."

Callie wiped imaginary sweat from her forehead. "Now that I know I'm safe, how about some of that cake?"

Lauren grabbed the box off the table and headed for the kitchen. "You read my mind, girlfriend. Be right back."

"Are these flowers from Kevin?" Callie asked, referring to the floral arrangement on the table.

"They came yesterday, and this morning he called to wish me a happy birthday." Lauren sliced into the dense cake and cut two large pieces. "You want some coffee, too?"

"All set thanks."

Lauren paused, a slice of cake hovering over the dish. "Did you just say no to coffee?"

"I had three cups on my way here. Do you have any of the herbal tea I had the last time I visited?"

"Sure. I bought a new kind, too, if you want that instead. It's orange spice."

"Nah, just give me the same one from before. I liked that one a lot. Actually, I bought some when I got home. So how are things going with Kevin?"

Lauren switched her thoughts over to Callie's question as she prepared the tea. Since she'd started seeing Kevin, she hadn't really discussed the budding relationship with anyone. "Okay. We're still getting to know each other." Lauren reentered the living room and handed Callie a plate and her tea.

Callie rolled her eyes. "Which means what exactly? Are you dating other people? Has he met your family? Come on, Lauren, I want details here."

Lauren swallowed the tiny bit of heaven in her mouth. "He'll meet them this weekend. He was supposed to come to Jenny's birthday party with me but didn't make it. Some emergency at work." It still bothered her a little that he had to work during her niece's birthday party after promising he'd come. "And I haven't been out with anyone else since our first date back in January."

Callie took a forkful of cake and then put her plate down. "I still cannot believe Jenny's three."

"Tell me about it." Lauren reached for her steaming mug of coffee. "It seems like she was just born yesterday."

"So, will Kevin be at your mom's retirement party tomorrow?"

"He promised he'd be there."

"I'm still surprised she's retiring. I thought she'd be there forever."

"It surprised everyone. She's worked in the school library for more than twenty years. The principal tried to change her mind, but Mom refused. She wants to be around when Kelly has the baby next month. When Kelly's maternity leave ends, Mom is going to watch the baby during the day." Lauren dug her fork into the cake again. "So, do you still love it at the academy?" After her marriage, Callie had decided to remain a teacher. A decision that had shocked the media and much of the country.

Callie raised another forkful of cake toward her mouth. "Most days. You know how it is. But I'm tossing around the idea of leaving at the end of the school year. Maybe taking on some charitable work instead. It'll be something different, and when Dylan travels I can go with him."

"How is he really? Has he been traveling a lot again?" Lauren had never met a worse workaholic than Callie's husband. While Callie said he was not as bad as when they'd first met, he still put in an obscene number of hours.

Callie rolled her eyes. "Busy as usual. You know him, but most weekends he leaves work at the office. He hasn't traveled since the end of January, but he'll be away for five days in April. I'm not looking forward to it."

"Yeah, but just think how happy he'll be to see you when he gets home," Lauren said in a suggestive tone.

Callie laughed and nodded. "He always is, but enough about him. What do you want to do tonight? It's your birthday; we should do something special. Something we haven't done together in a while."

The next several minutes they tossed around ideas before deciding on a movie followed by a late dinner. For a moment it felt like old times. That whole part of her life seemed like ages ago. While she loved seeing how happy Callie was with Dylan, she missed having her best friend just fifteen minutes away. Since freshman year in high school they'd been friends. They'd even taught at the same elementary school after college. Now she saw Callie perhaps once every six weeks or so. They talked on the phone frequently, but even their conversations had changed. They were not only in different places in their lives, but now their lives were rooted in different worlds. Even with all the differences between them, she still thought of Callie as a sister. And she knew Callie felt the same way. Sometimes, though, she wished they could go back to the way life was before Callie met Dylan, not that she would ever tell Callie that. Some things were best kept to oneself.

***

"Looks like Dylan has a new best friend," Lauren

said dryly. She and Callie sat together at a corner table in the banquet room of The Davenport on Saturday night. Callie's husband had arrived late that afternoon to accompany Callie to Mrs. McDonald's retirement party.

"I don't think Kevin has left him alone all night." Across the room, the two gentlemen in question stood at the bar getting drinks. Even from this distance she could see that Kevin was still talking while Dylan nodded in agreement.

"It does look that way. They're probably talking about debt to income ratios or some other business topic." Callie took a sip of her water. "Sometimes men like Kevin and Dylan need a little reminder that work is over."

"I guess. But I still can't believe Kevin got here so late tonight." She'd been prepared to drive herself to the party and leave a note for him on the door, when he finally pulled into her driveway. He'd lost track of time working on a project and then hit heavy traffic on the drive up from Rhode Island.

Callie leaned closer to her. "Then you just have to make sure he forgets about work sometimes. That's what I do." Callie gave her a devious smile.

Lauren burst out laughing. "You're evil, you do know that, girlfriend."

"But you love me anyway."

Lauren smiled and shook her head.

"How long is Kevin staying?"

"He leaves in the morning for Atlanta." She'd hoped he' would stay longer. They hadn't seen each other in almost two weeks.

"That stinks. He's staying with you tonight though, right?"

Lauren shook her head. "I invited him, but he said it'd be better if he stayed in the city tonight. His flight leaves early." His reasoning made perfect sense, and she hadn't tried to convince him otherwise. That didn't mean she wasn't disappointed.

"You weren't kidding when you said you two weren't serious yet."

This thing with Kevin was far from a serious committed relationship. Granted she hadn't dated anyone else since they'd met at the fundraiser, but she didn't know if the same was true for him. Neither had ever come right out and said seeing others wasn't allowed.

"You really need to start believing me, chickie." Lauren glanced down at her watch. "Mom should be here any minute."

"Does she suspect the party is for her?"

Lauren couldn't help but roll her eyes. "She knows. Kelly let it slip, but Mom's been playing along. I don't think anyone else knows that the surprise has been blown."

Scanning the room, Lauren made a mental list. It looked like everyone had made it. That didn't surprise her. Anyone who spent even five minutes with Virginia McDonald became her friend. Her kind and outgoing personality drew people to her and she was like a mother to every student who ever walked into the school library over the past twenty years. The room was filled to capacity with Virginia's friends and coworkers, as well as past and present students who wanted to wish her well in her retirement.

The main doors of the room opened as Lauren paused her scan; the guest of honor was about to enter. Grabbing her camera, Lauren stood—only to immediately collapse back down into her chair when her knees gave out at the sight of Nathaniel Callahan standing in the doorway.

"Oh my God." Her stomach hit the floor.

"What's the matter? Are you okay?" Callie's concerned voice sounded as if it were traveling a great distance to reach her.

Lauren glanced over at Callie and then toward the door again. Perhaps she'd imagined him. After all, why would he be here? The last time she'd heard anything about him, he was doing his third tour in the Middle East. Despite her hope that she'd started to hallucinate, when she looked again, he was still there, dressed in a black suit rather than his Marine uniform, his brown hair cut military short and looking much the same as he did the summer he'd broken her heart. She latched her hand onto Callie's arm. "Nate Callahan. He's here."

She kept her eyes on him. Since that awful day the summer after senior year, she'd only seen him once. She'd been home visiting her parents during holiday break her freshman year of college. She'd spotted him in his parents' driveway from her bedroom window. They'd received more than two feet of snow the night before and he was helping his father shovel. That morning she'd stood and watched until the entire driveway was cleared. When he and his dad finished, he went back inside his house without so much as a glance toward her home.

"What?" Callie asked, her voice louder than necessary.

Out of the corner of her eye, she saw Kevin and Dylan headed back to the table. "Nate just walked in," Lauren hissed.

"Lauren that . . ." Callie's voice trailed off and she sat up straighter. Her head moved to keep him in sight as he walked toward his parents. "What's he doing here?" she asked, her voice lower now.

Leaning closer, Lauren whispered, "I don't know. We don't exactly speak."

"They didn't have what you asked for, so I got this instead." Dylan sat down on the other side of Callie and placed a glass on the table.

"That's fine. Thanks." Callie wrenched her arm free from Lauren's vice-like grip. The movement pulled Lauren's attention away from Nate and back to her companions.

"Didn't you say the party started at five o'clock?" Kevin asked from her other side. "I'm surprised your mom isn't here yet."

Was that annoyance in his voice or had she imagined it? She couldn't tell for sure; her system was still in shock. Perhaps her emotions were making her hear things. "Guests were supposed to be here between five and six. My father planned to have my mom here around six." Determined not to focus on the party's unexpected guest, she turned her full attention toward Kevin. "They should be here any minute."

No sooner had she said the words than the lights flickered on and off in an attempt to get everyone's attention.

"They are on their way down the hall now," Kelly called out, standing near the front of the banquet room.

Practically as one, everyone not already standing came to their feet and turned toward the main doors. For the moment, Lauren pushed aside all of the swarming thoughts in her head. Tonight was a big night for her mom, and she wanted to enjoy it.

Again the door opened, this time Virginia and Thomas McDonald walked in. Immediately, the room erupted with a chorus of "Surprise!" followed by applause. Much to her credit, Virginia McDonald gave the best performance of her life. For a minute, even Lauren believed that her mom was surprised.

Wiping tears from her face, Virginia accepted the microphone the DJ held out to her. "I . . . I don't know what to say. Thank you all so much." Virginia handed the microphone back to the DJ, and then both she and her husband followed Kelly to the table of honor that had been set up near the front of the room.

Throughout dinner, Lauren tried to stay focused on the various conversations at the table, but nothing captured her attention. She remained fixated on the party's unexpected guest across the room while next to her, Callie and Kelly discussed Kelly's baby preparations, and across the table her older brother Matthew and Kelly's husband, Jared, discussed basketball. On her other side Kevin remained relatively quiet now.

"Lauren, it looks as if your mom will be missed. How long did she work at the school?" Dylan's mildly accented voice pulled her thoughts back to the table.

"If you count the five years she worked as a teacher before Matt was born, twenty-five years." Once again, Lauren glanced around the room. The last time she'd seen him, Nate had been walking toward the bar. Immediately she had looked down, afraid he'd spot her and guess she had been looking for him. But that had been at the beginning of dinner. Now only her aunt stood at the bar, most likely ordering her favorite drink, a nonalcoholic piña colada.

"I think she's going to miss it." She scanned the right side of the banquet room and spotted him. As if guided by radar her eyes locked on his profile. He was seated with his parents, and judging from the smiles on their faces, she guessed he was telling them some humorous story. He'd always been an excellent storyteller, even in elementary school. And when the two families would have campfires in the backyard during the summer or go camping together, he came up with the most imaginative tales.

A hand settled over hers and the sudden contact made her jump. "He wants to know if you're done eating," Kevin said, nodding toward the waiter standing at the table.

Had he asked her the same question already and she missed it?

"Yes. Thank you." Lauren handed the nearly full

plate to the young waiter and reached for her drink

"You've been distracted tonight. Are you okay? Something you want to talk about?" Kevin released her hand.

No not really. How could she tell her date (Or should she call him her boyfriend? She still wasn't sure what to call him.) that the man she'd once spent days dreaming about marrying was sitting on the other side of the room? And just the sight of him was making her heart rattle around in her chest. "Sorry, one of my students had some behavioral problems this week. I keep thinking about it." Her statement was not a complete lie. One of her students had received in-house suspension that week for starting a fight at recess.

"There is nothing you can do about it now, right? So relax and enjoy yourself. Everyone else is."

How many times now had he said things like that when she told him about problems at school? She tried to explain to him that as a teacher she couldn't leave work behind the same way people in other professions did. Each and every one of her students was important to her. She cared what happened to all of them.

"You never mentioned that Callie and her husband were coming tonight. Are they visiting you long?"

With a sigh Lauren shook her head. "They're going back to New York in the morning." She wished Callie were staying longer.

"Too bad. Next time they're in town we should all go out." Kevin wrapped his hand around hers, his signet ring digging into her skin. "Let's dance."

As soon as the wait staff began to collect the dinner plates, the DJ cranked up the music. Now, instead of classic instrumentals, Top 40 dance hits poured from the speakers and guests of all ages moved to the beat on the dance floor. Any other time she would've joined them out there immediately. Dancing was her first love. In fact, two nights a week she taught ballet at a nearby dance school. But now she held back. So far she'd managed to avoid Nate Callahan. They hadn't even made eye contact. For all she knew, he may not have even seen her. If she moved onto the dance floor, though, there'd be no hiding from him; she'd be too exposed.

He may not even care if he sees me. After all, he could have contacted her at any time during the past fifteen years, but he hadn't. Why would he bother with her now?

"I know you love to dance." Kevin stood. His slight tug on her hand forced her to concentrate on the here and now rather than what if.

"I do." She straightened her shoulders and stood.

The conversation between his parents faded into the background as Major Nathaniel Callahan once again scanned the crowd in search of the only person in the sea of familiar faces he needed to see. Leaving this room tonight without at least talking to Lauren wasn't an option for him. Unfortunately, so far she'd proved elusive, and with the evening half over it was time to be a bit more proactive in his search, which meant getting off his ass and mingling. Standing, he surveyed the crowded dance floor. Couples of every age moved to the slow ballad that poured from the speakers. Walking the perimeter, he avoided the dance floor. He had not stepped on one since his senior prom. He probably wouldn't have ventured onto it that night either if Lauren hadn't insisted. Dancing was one of things she'd always loved to do and one of the few things they'd disagreed on.

As he rounded the edge of the dance floor, his eyes zeroed in on a man and woman. Instantly, his feet slowed and his eyes studied every inch of the couple. He didn't recognize the man and dismissed him from his thoughts. The overhead lights reflected off the woman's ash-blonde hair, and excitement surged through him. While he couldn't see her face, every fiber of his body knew Lauren stood just feet away.

With his target in sight, Nate crossed the dance floor and reached the couple just as the song ended and a fast Top 40 dance hit came on. Something between anger and nausea rolled through him as the couple broke apart and the man whispered something in Lauren's ear. Then she turned and her eyes locked with his. Unable to look away, Nate held her gaze as a whole gamut of emotions swept through him. For the past year, everything he had done was in preparation for this moment. He'd tried to envision how their first meeting would go. Many scenarios had played through his head. Everything from passionate embraces to doors being slammed in his face. None, though, had included the utter fear on her face or the expensively dressed man with his arm around Lauren's shoulders. When she didn't make a move, Nate stepped toward her. In response, her date pulled her closer to his side.

"Lauren, I've been looking for you all night."

Lauren swallowed, her owl-sized eyes staring back at him as if he were a ghost.

"Nate . . . I didn't . . . what are you doing here?" she asked in that low, sultry voice he laid awake nights thinking about.

"Your mom invited me." No way in hell was he revealing anything in front of her date. "Evidently she knew about the party tonight." Not that he was surprised by that. Virginia McDonald always seemed to know everything that was going on in town.

Lauren nodded, her eyes never leaving his face. "I know. Kelly let it slip. You know her. But I think she convinced everyone else that she didn't know about the party when she walked in."

"I think you're right."

"Aren't you going to introduce us, Lauren?" Her date spoke to Lauren, but his eyes never left Nate's face.

Nate met his glare and waited for the other man to look away first. Something that didn't take him long to do.

Color spread across Lauren's face, turning her cheeks pink, and she looked over at her companion as if just remembering he stood there. "Sorry. Kevin, this is Nathaniel Callahan. We lived next door to each other until he joined the Marines." She paused and pressed her lips together. "Nate this is Kevin Walsh."

Her introduction told him little. She hadn't said her boyfriend, and there was no ring indicating this was a fiancé. He'd checked that already. Yet the way the man stood with his arm around her shoulders told him something existed between them.

"Nice to meet you." Nate stuck his hand out. When the other man didn't immediately respond, Nate's dislike of him increased.

"You, too." Kevin finally extended his free hand, but all the while he kept his arm around Lauren's shoulders.

You could tell a lot by someone's hands. For instance, Kevin's hands were soft. There were no calluses or old scars. Evidently he didn't work with his hands. His nails were even and he wore a large signet ring on his finger.

Clenching his jaw, Nate fought the urge to remove the arm from Lauren's shoulders. Right now all he could do was keep her talking. "Is Callie here tonight?" He hadn't seen her yet either, but it only made sense that she would be here. The two girls had been very close in high school. Thanks to the media, he'd seen pictures from Callie's wedding on the Internet and knew Lauren had been Callie's maid of honor, so he assumed they were still like sisters.

Lauren frowned but nodded. "She's here with her husband. If you want to say hello, she's still at our table on the other side of the room."

Everything from her body language to her voice told him she was uncomfortable. Yet his pleasure at finally seeing her kept him from letting her walk away.

After fifteen long years he wanted to stand there and soak up the sight of her.

"I'll catch her before I leave tonight."

"She'd like that." Lauren pressed her lips together and met his gaze. "How long are you on leave?"

"I'm not on leave, I'm back permanently." A room full of people prevented him from telling her everything, but he needed her to know he wasn't going anywhere. "Until I find a place, I'm staying in my parents' apartment."

An emotion he couldn't label flickered in her eyes and then disappeared. "Then I guess I'll see you around."

"Plan on it."

Lauren's lips started to form a word, but then she stopped herself.

"Didn't you want to check on your sister?" Kevin asked.

She nodded and looked over at her date. "I do," she said before her eyes met his again. "She wasn't feeling well earlier. It was nice seeing you tonight, Nate. I'm glad you came."

How could he argue with that? He'd seen Kelly earlier, and she looked as if she could have her baby any day now. "Tell her I said hello. And I'll see you soon."

Lauren graced him with a tentative smile. "I will." With her date's arm still around her, she walked away.

Another jolt of jealousy shot through Nate as she crossed the dance floor. Logically he realized he should've expected her to be involved with someone. Not once during their time apart had he contacted her or given her any indication he wanted a relationship with her. Still, he hadn't been prepared to see her with another man. Instead, he'd hoped that by some miracle she was waiting for him. The presence of a man in her life tonight changed nothing. While it might complicate his current mission, it didn't change it. Even with a guy in her life, he intended to fight for her.

***

He'd noticed the change in Lauren the moment Nate stopped them. Her back went rigid and she'd all but entirely clammed up. Even now, more than two hours since their run in, she remained unusually quiet. In the time he'd known her, she'd always kept up a steady conversation when they got together.

Readjusting his legs under the table in an attempt to get comfortable, Kevin shot a quick glance around the banquet room and shook his head. The party didn't look to be winding down anytime soon. Any other time he wouldn't have minded that, but he had work to finish tonight so he'd be prepared for his first meeting in Atlanta tomorrow. He'd worked on it already that afternoon before the party, but still had a fair amount to do. He couldn't tell Lauren that, though. He'd already messed up tonight by showing up late and didn't want any more strikes against him. They were still early on in their relationship, and if he hoped to keep things progressing toward an engagement, he needed to show her he was invested in them as a couple.

Kevin lifted his glass, prepared to finish off his drink, when his eyes locked on the guy from the dance floor Not that the guest Lauren introduced as Nathaniel Callahan noticed. Judging by the way the guy stared at Lauren now and the way she had reacted to him, they'd been more than just neighbors growing up. Putting his drink down, Kevin leaned in toward her and placed a kiss on her cheek. "Ready for another dance?" he whispered in her ear.

When Lauren jumped slightly, he clenched his teeth together as a light blush crept up her cheeks. Obviously, she'd been thinking about something other than him. Definitely not something that normally happened with women he dated.

"Um . . . sure. I'd like that."

Standing, Kevin pulled back Lauren's chair and took her hand. As she came to her feet, he shot another look in Nate's direction and nodded. In response, the guy's eyes narrowed and he scowled but then looked away.

Kevin led Lauren onto the dance floor as another slow ballad started. Pulling her close, he wrapped his arms around her, but his mind stayed focused on the guy across the room. Or rather how he was going to make sure he stayed away from Lauren. He hadn't spent the past few months developing this relationship with her just so someone from her past could come along and lure her away.

***

"Don't forget what I said. You can stay as long as you want. There's no need for you to rush out and find a place." Janet Callahan handed her son the keys to the apartment over the garage.

He'd only arrived back in town fifteen minutes before the start of the retirement party. Just enough time for him to run into his parents' house and toss on a suit. Now back at his parents' house, he was ready to collapse on the closest bed.

Yeah, there is. Nate kept the thought to himself as he accepted the keys. He'd come back to Massachusetts to start on the next phase of his life. He couldn't do that living over his parents' garage. Yet the apartment would provide him the perfect home base while he hunted for a new place. "I know, Mom." Nate started toward the door but stopped when he felt his mom's hand on his arm.

"I'm just so glad you're home for good this time." She wiped away the tears sliding down her cheek. "When you were over there . . . I was so scared."

Stepping back, Nate gathered his mother in his arms for a hug. He hated how much worry and fear his time in the Marines had caused his parents, especially his mother. Yet even knowing how much it had affected them, he didn't regret his years of service, right from the beginning at the Naval Academy. "It'll be different now that I'm in the reserves, Mom. I promise"

With a sniffle, Janet pulled away. "Make sure you come over for breakfast. I still make pancakes for your father on Sunday mornings."

"Sounds good." He pushed the door open.

"And Nate, thank you for coming to the party tonight. I know it meant a lot to Virginia that you were there."

He'd known Virginia McDonald all his life. Up until a few years ago, she and her husband had lived next door to his parents. "Wouldn't have missed it," he answered. And he meant it. In many ways, he viewed Virginia as a second mom.

"I saw you talking to Lauren. How did that go?" Her voice was gentle and understanding.

"We only spoke for a few minutes."

"I still believe you two belong together. I never understood what happened with you guys. But maybe you can finally work things out."

He'd never shared his reason for ending their relationship with anyone, and he didn't plan to start with his mother. "We'll see what happens." For now, that was all he intended to say. "I'll see you in the morning."

He let the door bang shut behind him and went straight to his Mustang for his bags before heading up the stairs to the apartment over the garage. Originally built for his grandparents when Nate's oldest brother was born, his parents now rented it out. And as luck would have it, right now the apartment was empty. The couple who had lived in it for the past three years had finally purchased a home of their own.

Unlocking the door, he turned the knob and walked inside. He couldn't remember the last time he'd stepped foot in the apartment, yet as he crossed the threshold, memories flooded back. Every day after school he'd come here and stay with his grandparents while his parents worked. His grandmother had taught him how to play the piano while his grandfather had taught him poker and chess. His grandparents moved out when he entered high school. Before his parents started renting the place out, he and his buddies from school would sneak in at night and have card games or sometimes drink beer.

Nate crossed the small kitchen and entered the furnished living room. Flipping on the light, another memory hit him as he stared at the open bedroom door. This time, though, it didn't involve his grandparents or his old high school buddies. This one involved him and Lauren. She'd not only been the girl next door but his girlfriend all through high school and up until he'd left for the Naval Academy after graduation.

They'd started out as childhood friends at the same preschool and had done lots of activities together. In elementary school, their interests led them into different activities. He'd been big into sports, while Lauren had spent hours dancing and taking voice lessons. Despite their different paths, they'd stayed close.

Then their last year of middle school things changed. No longer had he seen her as a pal. Instead, every time he looked at her his teenage body had gone into overdrive. Starting that summer until he left for the Academy they'd been an item. Together they'd experienced all the teenage firsts: first kiss, first time skipping school, first time having a drink—and first time having sex.

Staring at the bedroom door, it was that first his mind fixated on. It had been near the end of their sophomore year in high school. He'd picked her up at the private high school she attended, and they'd sneaked up to the empty apartment over the garage. Although they'd fooled around in the past, that particular hot May afternoon things went further than ever before. Soon they'd found themselves under the covers of the queen-sized bed.

In all honesty, it had been a less-than-epic occasion for both of them. He'd been all thumbs trying to get the condom on, and neither had really known what they were doing. Afterward, he'd been embarrassed by his performance or lack thereof, but she had not complained. Instead, she curled up next to him for the rest of the afternoon.

From that point on they talked about their future together as if it were a sure thing. But after his acceptance into the Naval Academy, he started to have doubts. Military families made unimaginable sacrifices every day, and deep down he'd known he couldn't ask her to do that. At the same time though, he'd known he had to go. The academy and the Marines would give him a chance to accomplish something significant, to make a difference. So, right before he left for Annapolis he'd ended things with her. From that day forward, the image of her face remained etched in his mind, despite all the time that had passed and all he'd seen as a Marine.

Nate rubbed a hand across his face in the attempt to dislodge the image of Lauren that summer day. Crossing to the bedroom, he dropped his bag on the bed and turned on his heel. Remembering the past accomplished nothing. All he could do was focus on the future, and thanks to Mrs. McDonald's retirement party earlier, he had begun working toward his goal and number one reason for requesting the Boston field office: winning Lauren back. A task perhaps more complicated than he expected.

He'd watched her and Kevin for the remainder of the evening. Yet he saw no conclusive evidence that her date was a significant part of her life. While Kevin kissed her once, he only did so when he caught Nate watching Lauren, almost as a way of marking his territory. And she never displayed any affection toward him. Whatever hope that gave Nate, though, got canceled by the fact she hadn't asked to see him again either. All she'd given him was a, "Maybe I'll see you around again." He wanted more than that from her. Then again, would she have said more with her date standing next to him?

Nate's reasoning squashed down the fear that he'd come back too late and reestablished his resolve. He'd been an idiot once and let Lauren go. Since that day, he'd never stopped regretting it. Now, with the change in his military status, he planned to do everything in his power to rectify that mistake.

Chapter 2

"I almost died when I saw Nate walk in the other night," Kelly said.

Join the club. Lauren reached out and accepted the curtain rod her sister held. "At first I thought I was seeing things."

"Well, if you have to see things, he wouldn't be a bad vision to have."

Lauren rolled her eyes. "And what are you doing noticing that, Kel?"

"I'm married, Lauren, not dead. Besides, it'd be hard *not* to notice him. Still, he had some nerve showing up."

She agreed with Kelly one hundred percent on that one. "It would've been nice to know he was

coming. Mom should have told me she invited him."
Lauren stepped off the stool and moved it over to the
other bedroom window.

"Maybe she wanted to surprise you."

"Mission accomplished if she did." She'd nearly
had a heart attack when she saw Nate walk in.

"So, what did he say to you? I saw him talking to
you and Kevin."

Lauren remembered every single word from their
brief conversation, but rather than rehash it all she
said, "Just hi and that maybe he'd see me around."

"That's it? I don't believe you."

Lauren's shoulders slumped. Her sister knew her
too well. Most of the time that was a good thing, but
every once in a while it really sucked.

"Every time I saw him his eyes were locked on
you. I think there's something you're not telling me,
Lauren."

Lauren sighed. "You're right." An image of Nate
that night formed in her mind. "When I said maybe I'd
see him around, he told me to plan on it." A shiver
went through her body, although whether from
anticipation or unease she wasn't sure.

Kelly's hand stilled, only half of the pastel yellow
curtain on the rod. "Interesting."

It took some self-control, but Lauren held back a
groan. She recognized her sister's tone. Kelly was
formulating some crazy plan or idea.

"He might be back for you, although I hope not.
He's the last person you need back in your life."

"Please. I haven't heard from Nate in fifteen

years. If he's moved back to Massachusetts it's not because of me, Kelly. " Lauren climbed up on the stool and waited.

"But what if it is?" Kelly handed her the curtain rod. "It's possible. I saw an article on the Internet about a couple who reconnected after thirty years apart."

Lauren hung the curtain in silence. Whatever plans Nate had, they didn't involve her. And she was okay with that. She had her own life and didn't need or want him back in it.

"Those are great stories, but they're rare. And I'm sure Nate's not looking to get back together. He's had plenty of time to do that. He came to the party because of Mom, and he's back here because his family is here." At one time she'd dreamed of nothing else. For more than a year after their breakup, she'd hoped that he'd come to his senses and reach out to her. Hundreds of times she'd envisioned him showing up at her door, once again telling her he loved her and wanted to be with her. Such a visit never happened. Eventually the dream faded and reality set in. She got on with her life, just as he had done with his.

"But what if he *is* back because of you?" Kelly lowered herself into the padded rocking chair near the crib. "If he showed up at your house tonight and told you he wants another chance, what would you do?"

Lauren tried to block the vision from forming by thinking of Kevin instead. Despite her best effort, Kevin's image disappeared and Nate's took his place. "I'd tell him it's nice to see him, but I'm with someone. Why would I want to risk what I have with Kevin for someone I haven't seen or heard from since high school?" Grabbing the waterproof mattress cover and sheet off the changing table, Lauren crossed to the crib. When she'd agreed to help with the final preparations in the nursery, she hadn't expected an interrogation as well. In retrospect, she should have expected it.

"Good. Nate doesn't deserve you," Kelly said curtly before switching gears. "I'm glad we got to meet Kevin. I liked him."

"Mom and Dad liked him, too." Lauren covered the mattress with the waterproof pad. "Do you think Mom had fun?"

Apparently not ready to talk about something else, Kelly ignored her sister's question. "How are things with Kevin? Do you love him?"

She held back a groan. It was always about love with Kelly. "No, not yet. We've only been dating a few months, Kel."

"And what about Neal, did you love him?" Kelly asked, referring to the pharmacist Lauren had dated the previous summer. "Or Marcus?"

Lauren tugged to get the sheet around the corner of the crib mattress. Maybe if she ignored her sister, Kelly would get the hint.

"What about Roger? Did you love him?" Kelly said, naming the last of the three men Lauren had dated in the last five years.

Annoyance and anger bubbled up inside Lauren. Dropping the mattress back into the crib, she spun on her heel. "I liked them all, you know that, but no, I didn't love them. If I had, I'd still be with one of them. So what's your point?"

Kelly rose from her chair, effort showing in her clumsy movement, and walked over to her. "Other than Nate, you've had one relationship that lasted more than nine months. And I think that's because you don't give any of them a chance. I think a part of you still loves Nate."

"Or maybe I just haven't met the right guy," Lauren shot back, reaching for the sheet again. "Who knows? Kevin might be the one."

With a sarcastic laugh, Kelly leaned her arm on the side of the crib.

"What's that cackle supposed to mean?"

"I don't think you'll give him a chance, either." Kelly shrugged. "He nice and I hope it works out, but . . ." Kelly's voice trailed off.

"But what?" Prior to this conversation, they'd talked very little about Kevin, or her love life for that matter.

"I think you will find something you don't like about him and end things."

"You're wrong."

Kelly placed a hand on her arm. "No, I'm not, Lauren, and I get it. I know how you felt about Nate. A person cannot simply get rid of feelings like that." Kelly's voice changed from her big sister know-it-all tone to her soothing therapist tone. "I think your love for him has kept you from falling in love with anyone else. But it's time to move past him. Really get on with your life."

Another denial sat on the tip of her tongue, but what was the point? Kelly was right, but only in part. Her inability to find love had nothing to do with Nate. She refused to believe that. No, she simply had not met the right man. Maybe this time with Kevin it would happen.

"Not that he plans on it, but even if Nate Callahan showed up tonight and asked me out, I'd say no." A tiny pain shot through Lauren's chest. Ignoring it, she continued. "And you're wrong. I am giving Kevin a chance."

"For your sake, I hope so. I think he could be the one."

Biting her lip, Lauren counted to five before speaking. She didn't want to argue with Kelly. "How about on this one we agree to disagree, okay? Arguing won't change whatever happens between Kevin and me."

With a loud sigh, Kelly nodded. "Fair enough, I guess. At least for now." She wrapped an arm around Lauren's shoulders. "How about we take a break in here? I picked up double chocolate chip brownies from Rosie's yesterday."

"You're just telling me this now? You should've brought those out the minute I walked in."

Lauren followed her sister into the kitchen. As they sat enjoying the chocolaty desserts from the town's best kept secret, they talked mostly about the upcoming birth of Kelly's first baby and the baby shower Kelly's co-workers had thrown for her.

Despite the pleasant conversation, Lauren's thoughts routinely drifted back to their conversation in the nursery. While what Kelly said was partially true, she'd never admit it aloud. On some level she'd never stopped loving Nate. She'd tried countless times to vanquish the feelings, but a tiny seed of love for him always remained. Eventually she'd assumed her residual feelings toward him were normal. They'd grown up together and he'd been her first love. Surely it was normal for your first love to always have a place in your heart. But regardless of what Kelly said, her inability to find love had nothing to do with Nate. It simply was a matter of not yet finding the right man. Just because Kelly had met and fallen in love with her husband while in college didn't mean everyone did. People met in all kinds of ways and at different times in their lives. Who knew? A year from now she and Kevin may be madly in love with each other. So what if she was not in love with him yet. She enjoyed spending time with him, and they had fun together. That type of relationship could easily turn into love. Not all relationships started off with fireworks.

Biting into the rich brownie, Lauren tried to picture herself with Kevin ten years from now. No matter how hard she tried, the visual wouldn't form. While she could picture herself several years from now sitting in her living room watching a movie while cuddled up next to someone, Kevin's face wasn't the one sitting beside her. Instead, Nate sat on the sofa, his arm around her.

Without stopping to consider what her actions

might tell her sister, Lauren popped the last bite of her brownie into her mouth and reached for a second. For years she'd kept thoughts of Nate Callahan blocked out, safely stored away. Now, though, she couldn't get him out of her head.

***

Nate pressed down on the accelerator of his Mustang as he hit the apex of the turn on Breakneck Hill and grinned. It'd been a long time since he'd driven the curvy road, but he still knew where each and every turn was. Man, it felt good to be home. Until the weekend before when he'd moved back into the apartment over his parents' garage, he hadn't realized just how much he'd missed Ridgefield.

Crossing over the town line into Slatersville, he turned onto Milford Road toward the center of town and Elm Street. He'd gotten Lauren's address from his mom the day after the retirement party. When he'd asked if she knew where Lauren lived, she hadn't asked any questions. Instead she'd given him a small smile, pulled out her address book, and wished him luck. He'd wanted to stop by that afternoon, but an appointment with a realtor made that impossible.

Turning right onto Elm Street, he slowed the car so he could check house numbers. All the homes on the street were either small capes or ranches with small yards. A few homes had swing sets or pools in the backyard, but for the most part it was your typical cookie-cutter neighborhood.

A mailbox with flowers painted on the sides and a large number four told him he'd reached his destination. Turning into the driveway behind a red Mini Cooper with a bumper sticker that read "Love to Dance," he killed the engine. Nervous energy shot through him as he studied the well-kept ranch before him. From the looks of it, the home had been recently painted, perhaps that past fall, and squat shrubs sat in a row in front of the farmer's porch. Right now the shrubs were still bare, but in the summer he imagined they'd be alive with color. A flagpole with an American flag was attached to the home and a black lamppost sat at the end of the brick walkway.

Getting out of the car, he slammed the door shut. Beneath his boots the gravel crackled as he strolled up to the walkway. The sound of a nearby wind chime and children playing outside a few houses down faded away as the blood thundering in his ears increased. Polite but distant described her behavior at the party. While she'd reacted much differently in his dreams, her initial reaction to his return didn't shock him, but it did disappoint him. A lot of time had passed since their last summer together. How would she react today?

Despite the cool temperature, a trickle of sweat ran down his back as he pressed the doorbell. Immediately, he heard a dog bark inside. As he waited, the dog inside continued to bark, but Lauren still didn't appear. Was she out? Had her date from the party come by and picked her up? With all the noise the dog made, she had to know someone was outside if she was home.

Damn it. He wanted to talk to her tonight. He'd already waited longer than he wanted. Inside, the dog became silent. Was it worth it to try the bell again? If his first attempt combined with the dog's racket hadn't told her she had a visitor, would a second attempt make a difference? On the other hand, he had nothing to lose by trying again.

Nate's finger zeroed in on the doorbell, but he stopped when Lauren opened the door. She was dressed in a long dark pink sweater with black leggings, and her ash blonde hair hung in a wet tangled mess around her shoulders. A black dog stood next to her, its tailing wagging back and forth. For a heartbeat or two, they both stared at each other, neither saying a word. Even with her uncombed wet hair and shell-shocked expression, she looked more beautiful today than she had when they'd dated.

"Nate?" Lauren's forehead creased. "What . . . why are you here?" She shook her head. "How did you know where I live?"

"I asked my mother." Starting with the simple questions seemed best.

"Oh. Yeah, I guess that makes sense."

Did she plan to invite him in? Standing in front of the open door with wet hair, she had to be cold. "Mind if I come in?" While he'd stand on the front step and talk all day if he had to, he figured they'd both be more comfortable inside.

Lauren blushed and took a step back. "Sorry. You surprised me. Come on in."

Although she let him, she didn't move from her new spot near the door or ask him to sit. "So, uh, what are you doing here?" Lauren pushed a clump of wet hair away from her face.

Nate glanced around the room briefly, searching for the right words before looking back at Lauren. Confusion and unease radiated from her expression. "I hoped we could talk," he said, wishing that he'd practiced what he wanted to say. "Catch up and stuff. I've missed you." Okay, so he'd never get a job writing romantic greeting cards, but he'd been honest with her.

Lauren frowned up at him. "Now isn't a good time. I'm getting ready to go out. When you rang the bell I was in the shower. I still need to fix my hair and do my makeup.

Jealousy exploded around his heart. "The snob from the party taking you out?" Nate tried to keep the anger from his voice, but the surprise on Lauren's face told him he'd failed.

"Kevin, my boyfriend, will be here soon."

He didn't miss the slight pause before she said "boyfriend," as if it was the first time she'd referred to him that way.

"We'll have to catch up some other time." Lauren added, her arms crossing over her chest. She glared at him.

Nate wanted to kick himself. This visit wasn't going the way he'd intended. "Lauren, I'm sorry. That was uncalled for." He took a step toward her, but stopped when her dog moved to sit directly in front of her. "I didn't come by to argue. I came here to talk. I hoped we could go out and catch up." Ignoring the dog standing guard, he took another step toward her. "I've missed you." Reaching for her hand, he intended to pull her arms away from her chest, but the moment he reached for her, she took a step back.

"You've missed me?" Lauren asked with disbelief. "How can you say that when not once in fifteen years did you contact me?"

Guilt slammed into him. "It's not that I didn't think about it."

"Thinking and doing are two different things, Nate," she said. Her light brown eyes narrowed and her voice turned cold.

Prepared to apologize, Nate opened his mouth but the doorbell rang, and he didn't get the opportunity to say anything. Once again the dog barked wildly as Lauren groaned and threw up her hands.

"Great. Kevin's here, and I'm not ready." Without another glance in his direction, she walked around him to the door.

As if this visit weren't already going downhill fast, now he had her boyfriend, or whatever he was, to contend with too. Turning toward the door, he watched her welcome Kevin inside.

"I'm running a little behind." She closed the front door behind Kevin. "You remember Nate from the other night." She nodded in his direction. "He stopped by to say hello."

Nate glanced back and forth between Lauren and Kevin. So far, neither had shown any display of affection. Not a hug or a kiss? Strange. Either the two of them were only friends despite Lauren's claims otherwise, or their relationship was still in its early stages. Both options worked for him, although the first could make his task much easier.

"Nice to see you again." Kevin extended his hand.

"Nate was just leaving," Lauren said before he could say or do anything. "Give me ten minutes, and we can leave too." Lauren took a step toward him. "Thanks for stopping by. It was good to see you." Lauren clasped her hands behind her back as she met his gaze. "Sorry we couldn't talk longer."

The confusion and apprehension in her eyes betrayed her true feelings. She obviously wanted him as far away from her as possible right now.

"That's okay. We'll catch up some other time." He took a step back toward the door. *Retreat.* The word rolled through him along with disgust. He wasn't the kind of man who retreated. Yet at the moment he had no other option. She'd made that quite clear.

***

The theater exploded in another roar of laughter when Lisa Jones, the comedian on the stage, delivered the punch line. Lauren, however, remained silent. She had missed the first half of the joke, so the punch line made no sense to her. Actually, so far that night, she'd missed most of the jokes. Sure, she'd heard the comedian's words, but she hadn't processed most of them. Instead, her thoughts returned time and again to her past two conversations with Nate.

When she'd opened the door that night, her first instinct had been to throw herself against him and wrap her arms around him. But that emotion quickly changed, and the urge to slam the door in his face took over. Thanks to sheer willpower, she'd avoided doing both.

Who did he think he was just dropping by like that? He could have called first. His mother, also her boss now that she'd become principal at the elementary school, not only had her address, but also her cell phone number. How could he think she'd believe his line about missing her? He'd been the one to end things all those years ago, not her. She would've stayed with him as he went through the Naval Academy and whatever else the Marines required from him.

A smooth warm hand settled over hers, and Kevin's breath spread across her cheek. "Did you hear me?"

Lost in her own thoughts, she'd tuned out the rest of the room, including her date. "Sorry. I'm a little tired tonight." She gave him a small smile. "I spent most of yesterday helping Kelly decorate the nursery, and then I worked on this week's lesson plans."

The house lights overhead came up, filling the refurbished turn-of-the-century theater with light. "There's a fifteen- minute intermission. The cafe probably has some decent coffee."

"Sounds good." Lauren stood.

Kevin kept a hand at the small of her back as they weaved through the crowded theater. Judging by the long lines outside the restrooms most patrons were making a bathroom stop before doing anything else.

"Your sister is due soon, right?"

They'd had this conversation twice already. How could he have forgotten again? "Three weeks." Lauren sat down at a covered table.

"What do you think of the show?" Kevin took the seat next to her and handed her a coffee.

"Great," Lauren said, although she didn't have an opinion. So far she'd managed to miss the entire thing. "Lisa Jones is hilarious. I don't know how she manages to keep a straight face." At least the few times she'd seen her on television she'd managed to get out the most over-the-top jokes without cracking a smile. Why would tonight be any different?

Kevin draped an arm across the back of her chair, his hand brushing against her arm. "I preferred Carl Patterson myself. I thought Lisa's jokes bordered on redneck territory."

Lauren shrugged. Truthfully, when she'd seen the show performed on a cable comedy channel, she'd much preferred Lisa's down-to-earth comedy to Carl's politically laced humor. Yet it didn't shock her that Kevin either didn't or couldn't appreciate Lisa's jokes. Even before the last two comedians went on tonight, she could guess which one he'd favor. The four comedians had been touring for years together and had done many television specials despite their different styles.

"Are you driving back to Providence tonight?"

Kevin sipped his latte. "No, I'm heading to my parents for the night. I have a meeting in Boston tomorrow morning, so I figured I'd stop in to say hello and spend the night."

Ah yes, his elusive parents. They'd been dating for months now, and she still hadn't met them, even though their estate in Weston was less than an hour from her house. She'd hinted at wanting to meet them, but so far he'd not caught on. Or maybe he didn't want her to meet them. Every time she thought that, she pushed the idea away. Still, the more time that passed, the more it popped up.

Lauren once again pushed the unpleasant thought away. One of these days she'd meet his parents. "Does that mean you'll be around this week?"

"Unfortunately, no. After my meeting, I'm flying to Dallas for a few days."

Holding back a sigh of disappointment, she reached for her coffee. How did Callie do it? Dylan traveled a lot. Even early in their relationship when they'd done the long distance thing, Callie hadn't complained. Yet it drove Lauren insane. Trying to make a long distance relationship work was difficult enough, but adding in Kevin's frequent travel made it harder.

"But I'll be back in Providence late Friday night. Why don't you come down Saturday morning and spend the weekend?"

Something akin to giddiness swept through her. He'd never before invited her to the city to visit him.

Instead, he always made the trip up to her. "I'd love to."

Leaning closer, Kevin kissed her cheek, the musky cologne he wore wrapping around her. "Excellent. If they're not busy, perhaps Callie and her husband would like to join us for dinner Saturday night. We could meet them halfway."

Over the theater's intercom, a bell rang signaling the end of intermission. "I'll check with her." In all honesty, she didn't want them to have dinner together. Sure she adored Callie and thought Dylan was a great guy, but considering the amount of time she and Kevin got together, she didn't feel like sharing him. But as they headed back into the theater for the remainder of the show, she pushed all the negative thoughts away. Kevin had asked her down to the city. It appeared as though their relationship was taking a more serious turn.

Chapter 3

Nate rounded the corner of Main Street and Union, his feet pounding the sidewalk. At the end of the leash, Maggie, the Boxer-Lab mix he'd adopted earlier that week, ran along beside him. He'd grown up with a dog in the house. During his time in the Marines he'd missed the constant companionship a dog provided and promised himself he'd adopt a dog as soon as he settled in back home. The night after he confronted Lauren, he'd stopped in the local animal shelter. After hearing the story of how Maggie had been abandoned at a truck stop, he'd taken her home. While the shelter workers claimed the young dog was leery of strangers and had possibly been abused by her previous owner, she'd immediately taken to Nate.

Since coming home with him, she hardly left his side when he was around.

If only he could win over another female as easily. His last conversation with Lauren had been a disaster. She'd made it clear she didn't want him back in her life. Lauren had moved on without him. And while a part of Nate urged himself to fight for her, to not give up on them being a couple again, he saw no other option at the present time.

Continuing on Union, Nate waved back at Mr. Crooks, his seventh grade gym teacher, who pulled grocery bags out of his car. Like many in New England, it looked as if the former gym teacher had picked up some extra food in preparation for the rare late winter storm the meteorologists were predicting for tomorrow. A few houses down, he glimpsed Steven Fowler and his son tossing a football around in the front yard. He'd run into his former high school buddy earlier in the week and had been shocked to learn that the guy had a son. Of all the guys he'd hung with in high school, Steven Fowler was one of the last he'd expected to see with a child.

With a throw reminiscent of his days playing high school football, Steve tossed the ball back to his son at the far end of the yard and waved in Nate's direction.

Nate nodded and waved but didn't stop as he approached the house.

"I expect to see your ass here tomorrow night for the Celtics game," Steve called out when Nate got within hearing.

Nate nodded again and turned the corner. In high

school he, along with Steve Fowler, Ben Fitzgerald, and Mitch Johnson, had always hung together. They'd played on the same teams and always gathered to watch their Boston sports teams on television. While he'd lost touch with his buddies, they had stayed tight over the years and still got together regularly. When he'd run into Steve, the guy immediately invited him to join them for the Celtics game as if no time had passed.

But time had passed. A lot of time. Damn it. At eighteen he'd had it all figured out. Before he and Lauren started their life together, he wanted to accomplish something. Be a part of something that was bigger than himself. So he'd applied to the Naval Academy in Annapolis. In his mind he'd get a degree from the Naval Academy and then serve with the Marines before joining the reserves and coming back for Lauren. And in his self-absorbed eighteen-year-old mind, she would be waiting for him. Then 9-11 happened and destroyed his well-ordered plan. He couldn't let his fellow Marines, his brothers, fight and die while he returned home. So he remained and convinced himself Lauren would still be there. That she would forget the past and welcome him back as if no time had elapsed.

How fucking conceited could I be? Maybe, just maybe if he'd let her in on his plan or had come back even a few months earlier he would have had a chance. He hadn't, though, and now he had to live with his decisions. Anger raged inside him as he continued down Lincoln before crossing onto Fairview Street toward his parents' home. Without pausing, Nate jogged up the wooden stairs to the apartment over the garage, Maggie panting heavily behind him. The run had been an excellent way to get back into his exercise regimen. Over the past week he'd slipped out of his routine. The need for exercise hadn't been what had sent him out, though. Exercise in general and especially running usually helped calm him. Yet tonight it hadn't. In fact, he felt angrier now than before he left because he realized that while he wanted to get past the wall Lauren threw up between them, he needed to respect her wishes. He couldn't force her to let him back into her life. The best he could hope for right now was a change of heart on her part.

***

Lauren wiped her feet on the welcome mat and closed the door behind her. "Jared call you back yet?" she asked when she spotted her sister across the room.

"He's meeting us at the hospital," Kelly said, her face contorted with pain.

"Do you have everything you need?"

Kelly nodded as she gripped the back of a chair and groaned. "My bag has been packed for two weeks now."

"Let's go, then." Lauren snatched her sister's jacket off the coat tree and pulled open the door. "Is this your bag?" she asked, pointing to the small suitcase on the floor. When Kelly nodded, she grabbed it. "Be careful. The stairs are a little slippery," Lauren called over her shoulder. The concrete stairs were coated with about an inch of snow. According to yesterday's forecast, the rare late March snowstorm was only supposed to drop about three to four inches of snow, but judging by the way it was coming down, she expected the estimate to go up.

"I cannot believe it is snowing. It's almost the end of March."

"Yeah, well, it looks like everything is on its own time schedule this year." Lauren opened the car door for her sister. "The baby isn't supposed to be here yet, either."

After Kelly made herself as comfortable as possible in the passenger seat, Lauren slammed the door closed and walked around to the other side. "I hope you and Jared decided on names finally." Lauren pulled out onto the deserted street that hadn't yet been touched by a plow. The last time she'd asked, her sister and brother-in-law still had not narrowed down their original list of fifteen names.

"We picked Patrick if it is a boy, and if it's a girl it'll either be Beth or Alexa."

Lauren kept up a steady stream of chatter during the long ride from Kelly's to the hospital. Most days the ride from Kelly's house to the hospital only took about ten minutes. Today the ride took almost twenty because it seemed as if every nervous driver in Massachusetts was on the road. "You would think these people have never seen snow. I could walk to the hospital faster than this," Lauren complained, once again stuck behind a slow-moving car. In the distance, she could see the hospital. "There's sand on the road already, it's not that slick."

"You know how some people get," Kelly said, sounding short of breath.

"You're doing great. Hang in there." Lauren pulled into the hospital driveway but drove past the parking garage and headed straight for the front entrance and valet parking. She opened the door while putting the car into park. "I need a wheelchair," she called out. Immediately, the young parking attendant, who had approached the car, bolted into the hospital as another came around to help Kelly into the wheelchair.

"You ready to do this?" Lauren asked, pushing her sister through the glass doors and into the hospital's lobby.

Kelly groaned in response, her arms crossed around her middle.

Without pausing, Lauren moved toward the elevators. "I'll take that as a yes. What floor?"

"Third," Kelly said, her voice somewhere between a groan and a whimper.

An hour later, Lauren sat in Kelly's hospital room where she would eventually give birth and stay for a few days. So far though, not much had happened. After checking in, the doctor on duty had done a quick exam. A nurse had hooked up a monitor to track the baby's heartbeat then left. So far, no one had returned. From the window, Lauren could see that the snow had picked up. And although she didn't say anything, she feared Jared might not make it to the hospital in time. Her sister had always known that was a possibility. Jared worked near Springfield about an hour away, and even when the weather cooperated, traffic could make the trip twice as long. For that very reason, Lauren had gone to the birthing class with Jared and Kelly. But while Kelly may have prepared herself for Jared not being there, she would be heartbroken if he wasn't.

"Do you want me to call Mom and Dad?" Lauren asked, turning her back on the window. Watching the snow would not make it stop. "Or do you want to wait until the baby is born?"

"After. I don't want them trying to get here in this storm, and you know they would." Kelly repositioned herself in the bed. "I don't want you to leave, but maybe you should head out now before the roads get really bad."

Lauren reached for her sister's hand. "I'll go as soon as Jared gets here." As much as she hated the idea of waiting until the roads got worse, she wasn't leaving her sister all alone either.

"He . . ." Kelly stopped as another contraction tore through her. "Who knows when he'll get here? I'll be okay. I'll worry less if you start home now."

"You're not getting rid of me that easily, Sis." Reaching for the remote, Lauren turned on the television and flipped through the limited stations. "As soon as Jared gets here, I'll go. I promise, okay?"

She made it through the first half of the evening news before her normally calm brother-in-law raced into the room. Jared's hair stood on end as if he'd spent the last few hours running his hands through it.

His tie had been loosened and left to hang at an odd angle around his neck. Without pausing, Jared rushed to his wife's side and kissed her. Then tearing off his jacket he tossed it onto the other empty chair in the room and turned toward Lauren. "The roads are shitty already and every idiot driver is out there."

On the drive over they had been a little slick but nothing she couldn't handle. Lauren had lived in New England all her life, so this was hardly her first snowstorm. But for Jared to complain, they must be really awful. He'd lived up in Bangor, Maine, for several years before moving to Massachusetts, and the winters up there were much worse than here.

Lauren leaned over to give her sister a hug. "Now that Jared's here, I will go. One of you better call me right after the baby is born, though. I don't care what time it is." Coming around to the other side of the bed she gave Jared a hug, too. "I mean it, right after."

Only after getting a promise that they'd call, Lauren left. As she waited for the valet attendant to bring around her car, she watched the fat snowflakes swirling through the sky. The few cars and trucks on the road were moving slowly, their windshield wipers fighting the trail of salt left behind as a large snowplow cleared a path down the road. Why did her sister's water have to break tonight? Yesterday would have been a much better day. She may do it every year, but she hated driving in the snow. She didn't mind a snowstorm once it ended and the roads were clear, but during the storm itself, well, that she hated

"Drive carefully, ma'am," the valet said before

closing Lauren's door for her.

With both hands, Lauren gripped the steering wheel, her knuckles turning white as she eased onto the street toward the highway. Though well into rush hour, the traffic on the road remained light.

Cranking up the windshield wipers, she turned the car onto Route 3. So far she'd seen two accidents and had slipped on ice twice. Both times her car's ABS brakes kicked in, bringing the car to a stop before she ran through the stop signs. That was the good news. The bad news was, she was only halfway home. Up ahead another stop sign appeared like a bright red beacon in the white snow. A gust of wind swept over the car, nearly blinding her. Taking in a slow steady breath, she pried her hands from the steering wheel when the car stopped. For a second, she thought she heard a grating sound sort of like metal rubbing against metal.

It's your imagination. After wiping her hands on her pants, she gripped the steering wheel and crossed the intersection. Once again the grating sound rumbled through the car. *That's not my imagination.* Lauren knew next to nothing about cars, yet even she recognized the sound as a bad sign. *Just let me make it home.*

The farther she drove, the louder the sound became. Then about a half mile down the road she finally pulled over. Driving the car the way it sounded couldn't be safe. Of all the nights for her car to act up it had to be tonight in the middle of a snowstorm. At least she'd gotten Kelly to the hospital. Now she had herself to worry about. Ever since she'd started driving, she'd belonged to MAA, Massachusetts Automobile Association. In the event of a breakdown or flat tire, they'd come out and either tow the car or fix it so she could get it to a garage. She didn't use it often, but whenever she did she was grateful for the service. Lauren pulled out her cell and dialed the number. After several rings a male voice answered.

"It may be a while before we can get to you," the operator said, after Lauren explained the situation. "We have had numerous accidents requiring tows. Sit tight, and we will get to you as soon as we can."

Sit tight? As if she had much of a choice. It wasn't as if she could run out and get a coffee. "Any idea how long it might be?"

"Minimum of an hour."

"Thank you." After all, what else could she say? Complaining wouldn't make a tow truck appear any faster. With a flick of her wrist, Lauren tossed the phone back into her bag and leaned between the bucket seats to reach the sweatshirt in the backseat. She'd thrown it back there so she could take it to school on Monday to keep in her closet. Now, though, the extra layer would come in handy. The heat had only been off for a few minutes, but already the temperature in the car was dropping.

Nate kept his speed a good ten miles per hour below the speed limit as he drove down Route 3 toward home. The high winds combined with the heavy snowfall made visibility poor. Yet he didn't mind the storm, or at least he wouldn't once he made it home. It had been a while since he'd experienced a good New England snowstorm. Outside, the headlights of his Mustang illuminated a red Mini with a 'Love to Dance' bumper sticker on the back. He knew that car. After all, how many red Minis could there be in the area with a bumper sticker like that? Not many. And even if it wasn't Lauren, whoever it was needed help. No person in his right mind . . . or her right mind . . . would be pulled over for fun on a night like this. Without any hesitation, Nate pulled up behind the parked car, put his in neutral, and approached the tiny car.

The inside of the Mini was dark, but through the driver-side window he could make out Lauren huddled in the front seat with her arms wrapped around herself. What had she been thinking to come out tonight? The conditions downright sucked. No one should be out unless absolutely necessary. If he'd known they'd get this bad on his way home, he would've camped out at the office tonight. Without considering what Lauren's reaction might be, he rapped his knuckles on the window. Immediately, Lauren's body jumped and her head whipped around toward him. The look on her face went from fear to shock and finally relief.

"What the hell are you doing out here?" Nate demanded once she opened her car door.

"Kelly needed a ride to the hospital. On the way home the car started making a god-awful sound. Now it won't start at all. I'm waiting for the tow truck, but they're very busy tonight." She rubbed her hands up and down her arms.

Nate took a step forward prepared to wrap his arms around her and keep her warm, but he stopped himself just in time. He'd lost the right to touch her a long time ago, and he may never earn it back. Her behavior the other night at her house proved that much. "How long have you been out here?"

Lauren pushed up her sleeve to check her watch. "About fifteen minutes. They said it would be at least an hour before they got here."

"Come on, you can wait in my car until they get here, and then I'll drive you home."

Lauren didn't argue. She grabbed her things and followed him back to his car. After they were both inside, he cranked up the heat. Though she hadn't complained, she looked half-frozen.

"Thanks for stopping," Lauren said as she spread her hands out in front of the air vents.

"Anytime. Is Kelly okay? Did she have the baby?"

"Not yet. At least when I left the hospital she hadn't. Her water broke earlier tonight, so I think she will have the baby soon. Jared promised to call after the baby is born."

Turning down the heat to keep from melting, he said, "Your parents must be excited. This is their second grandchild, right?"

"Third. Matt has two kids. Jenny just turned three, and Connor is almost six."

"My nephew turned six this month."

Lauren reached out and readjusted an air vent. "I know. David and Connor are both in Mrs. Parker's kindergarten class."

"I can't believe that woman is still there." Mrs. Parker had already been a veteran teacher when they'd been in her class.

"I think she just enjoys teaching, and she's good at it. All the kids love her. Even the ones that don't get her as a teacher."

"She was one of my favorite teachers," Nate said. "Do you remember that puppet she used when she read stories?"

For the next hour they shared their good and bad memories from elementary school. When flashing lights finally pulled up in front of Lauren's car, Nate reached for the door. "Looks like the tow truck is here."

"It's about time. I've never had to wait this long before for them to come."

Quickly the tow truck driver attached Lauren's car to the truck. After giving her the name of the garage he was towing it to, he pulled away from the curb, once again leaving them alone.

"We should go."

When Nate opened the car door for her and, as he headed down Route 3, they didn't speak at all. Under different circumstances he would've tried to get her talking again. Their earlier conversation had been relaxed and enjoyable. For the time being, however, he decided his concentration should be on the road rather than words. The road conditions had deteriorated while they'd waited for the tow truck and visibility stunk. Once he got her home safely maybe they could talk. Or perhaps he could talk and, hopefully, she'd listen. Since his visit to her house, he'd decided to honor her request and not bother her again—and hope maybe miracles did exist. But with Lauren so close now, he found himself wondering if he should try just one more time. During his last attempt he'd only scratched the surface of what he wanted to tell her before her date arrived.

Nate's blood started to boil at the thought of Lauren with her date. Where had they gone that night? What had they done when they returned? Nate clenched his jaw at the questions. None of it was any of his business. Acknowledging the fact didn't undo the knots in his stomach.

"I really appreciate the ride home," Lauren said, breaking the silence in the car for the first time. "I don't know what I would've done otherwise."

"Glad I could help." The car skidded to the right as he turned onto her street. Almost all of the houses were ablaze with light. It seemed as if everyone had decided to hunker down for the night and wait out the storm at home. In fact, Lauren's house was only one of two houses that didn't have lights on.

"JoJo is going to love going outside in this. I've never seen a dog like the snow as much as she does."

Speaking of dogs, he should probably call and ask his mom to let Maggie out. He'd been gone for hours, and who knew how long it would take him to get home. Before he left Lauren's he'd call. Although, knowing his mom, she had probably already stopped in his apartment to let the dog out and feed her.

"If you need a ride to the garage, call me." Nate stopped in front of her garage. She'd probably call Kevin or Kyle or whatever the guy's name was, but he wanted her to know he was there for her, too.

Lauren pushed open the door but didn't move. "You shouldn't be driving anymore tonight."

"I'll be fine."

Cocking her head to one side she looked at him then glanced out the window. "Why don't you stay here tonight? The roads are lousy, and I have a spare bedroom."

He'd envisioned spending the night with her many times over the years, but none of those visions ever included him using a spare bedroom. "You sure Kyle won't mind?" he asked, taking a guess at the guy's name.

"His name is Kevin, and no he won't mind." Lauren pushed the door open more. "I'll run in and open the garage door so you can park in there." She didn't wait for a reply. Jumping out, she trudged across the snow-covered walkway and into the house. Seconds later, the garage door went up, and Nate drove inside.

When he'd left work hours earlier he'd cursed the slow traffic leaving the city and the weather. Now, sitting in Lauren's garage, he didn't mind it so much. By nature Nate didn't buy into the whole everything-happens-for-a-reason belief. Yet, at least in this case, events out of his control were throwing the two of them together for the night. And even though he'd told himself to back off and leave her alone, he planned to make one last attempt at breaching her defenses.

Keep cool and don't let anything she says get your temper going. She'd always known how to get him going. When they'd been a couple, he'd sworn she did it sometimes just for fun.

Nate entered the house through the door connecting the two-car garage to the kitchen. On his last visit he hadn't made it any farther into the house than the living room, but he wasn't surprised that the kitchen reflected Lauren's personality. The walls were painted a sunny yellow, her favorite color. A few flowerpots overflowing with fresh herbs lined the windowsill above the sink. Bar stools sat beneath the counter, and pictures of famous locations in France hung on the walls. "Lauren," he called out, closing the door behind him.

"Make yourself at home. I'll be there in a minute."

Too bad you don't really mean that. If not for the storm and bad driving conditions, she would have sent him on his way as soon as they pulled into her driveway.

Nate made his way into the cozy living room and toward the couch. By the looks of things she'd left in a hurry earlier that night. A half-eaten sandwich and a glass of what he would bet his entire savings was root beer sat on the coffee table. Several textbooks lay open on the couch and a plan book was set next to them. Avoiding the books, he sat down and looked around the room. A large-screen television hung over the fireplace and two overstuffed chairs sat in front of a big bay window overlooking the front yard. A tall bookcase stood in the far corner. The bottom two shelves contained cookbooks, while the top three held framed photos. In this room, like the kitchen, she'd hung pictures of places in Europe she had always talked about visiting someday as well as a plaque that read, "Always Dance In The Rain."

Had she managed to travel to any of the places pictured on her walls? He could still vividly remember her talking about the trips she wanted them to take someday when they both graduated from college. If she had, whom had she taken with her? Had she traveled alone? Had Callie gone with her? The two of them were like sisters, or at least they had been. Had they traveled across Europe before Callie's marriage?

"Sorry, I needed to call Kevin back." Lauren put a little extra emphasis on his name as she came into the room. "I was supposed to drive down to Rhode Island tomorrow for the weekend."

She took a seat across from him, and Nate wondered why she was telling him all this, and if she'd told Kevin he was here. Could it be her way of telling him again that she had someone in her life and for him to leave her alone? Or was she just making polite conversation?

"By tomorrow afternoon the roads should be fine," he said, as visions of Lauren with Kevin formed in his mind.

Lauren nodded in agreement, causing a strand of

hair to fall forward. "I know, but I'll want to visit Kelly and the baby when he or she is born."

The reason for Lauren's dangerous trip out into the snow had slipped his mind entirely. "Have you heard from her or Jared yet?"

"No. I keep checking my text messages, but so far nothing," she answered, clear disappointment in her voice. "Are you hungry? There's a decent chance I'll lose power. It happens during almost every snowstorm, so if I'm going to cook I should do it soon."

"Sounds good. Whatever you have is fine."

Without a word, Lauren stood and went into the kitchen. Left alone, Nate moved over to the bookcase and the framed photos. The top shelf contained three: the one in the center of the shelf was of Lauren and Kelly at her sister's wedding, to the right was one of Lauren with her brother Matt the day he got married, and to the left stood one of Callie and Lauren at Callie's wedding. Several pictures of kids that he guessed were her niece and nephew filled the second shelf. Both children bore a resemblance to her brother. The last shelf contained a mixture of pictures of Lauren and her family. In some of them Lauren looked to be only five or six, while in others she was much older.

Tucked close to the back, one particular picture caught his attention. Pushing aside some frames, he grabbed the one almost hidden behind the others. In the picture, a nine-year-old Lauren stared back at him. She stood on the beach with Kelly and Matt on one side of her and Nate and his older brother Ryan on the other side. Behind the group stood Virginia McDonald and his mom and lying in front was the family dog. He remembered the exact moment her father took the picture. The two families had gone up to New Hampshire for a week together. It had been the first of many trips they had taken to New Hampshire together. Before that, they had always gone to a campground near Wells Beach in Maine. That year they had decided to try out a new location, and it had become a favorite for everyone.

He hadn't thought of those joint family trips in years. Now though, he could picture the sand castles they had built together and the hours they'd spent splashing in the lake or hiking along sections of the Appalachian Trail. Once it grew dark or the bugs got too annoying, they'd returned to their campers and played board games or told stories until their parents wrangled them into bed.

For years, going up there with his family and the McDonalds had been the highlight of his summer. Something he'd started looking forward to as soon as they had changed the clocks in the spring.

Nate placed the photo back on the shelf and glanced over the other framed pictures again. The picture of her and him on the beach with their siblings was the only one of its kind. All the others, with the exception of the one with Lauren at Callie's wedding, contained only family. There weren't any pictures of her and Kevin on the shelf, or anywhere else in the room for that matter. This photo must have meant a lot, otherwise it wouldn't have earned a spot on the bookshelf.

Did she often think about the trips they'd taken back then? Did she think about him? Over the years he'd spent countless nights unable to sleep with thoughts of her on his mind.

"Everything's ready. What do you want to drink?" Lauren appeared at the entrance, and he once again focused on the here and now.

"Do you have any soda?"

"Only root beer."

Just like he'd guessed. "That's fine." Nate stuffed his hands in his pockets to keep from reaching out for her and followed her into the kitchen. "Have you lived here long?"

"Almost two years." She made no attempt to elaborate as she grabbed a root beer from the refrigerator and handed it to him. "I need to go shopping, so there weren't many options for dinner." She settled herself on a bar stool at the counter.

Considering some of the food he'd eaten while in the military, she could have served him toast with butter and he wouldn't have complained. He nodded toward the grilled cheese and tomato sandwich and soup. "This is great. Thanks." Picking up his sandwich, he bit into it. Immediately his jaw froze as the rich combination of sharp cheddar, tangy tomato, and fresh basil exploded on his tongue.

She remembered. She'd never liked basil on her grilled cheese. When they'd been children she'd always reminded his mom not to add it to her sandwich when she cooked them grilled cheese. Yet his had some on it now. His heart smiled at the fact as he reached for the bowl of soup.

Bite. Chew. Swallow. Lauren went through the motions, while next to her Nate polished off one sandwich and started on his second. With him so close, she could hardly breathe, never mind eat. Ever since the retirement party, thoughts of him invaded her mind in a way they hadn't in years. But when she'd looked into the living room while preparing dinner and saw him holding that picture, an entire avalanche of feelings and memories dropped on her. For a brief moment she was once again a child on vacation with her family and best friend. Then her mind fast-forwarded to lazy summer days as a teenager with the person she'd thought she would spend the rest of her life with. Finally, she crashed headlong into the day he stood before her and crushed her heart.

Had he felt anything when he saw the picture? A tiny cruel part of her hoped he felt pain when looked at it. She still did, even after all this time. The picture also brought back memories of her wonderful childhood with the people who had played an integral part in it. For that reason she'd never gotten rid of the picture. She sometimes pushed it farther back on the shelf, when the memories of Nate's betrayal overshadowed the happy ones, but she never removed it.

"I'm going to change and send Jared a text message. Help yourself to anything in the refrigerator." Leaving her half-eaten dinner behind, Lauren escaped to her bedroom. Thanks to the combination of Nate's closeness and the painful memories stirred up by that picture, her ability to hold it together was near the breaking point. Anger and sadness clutched at her heart, and she wanted to yell at him for what he'd done all those years ago. Demand answers to the questions that had haunted her since then. But she knew doing those things would accomplish nothing. What happened back then was ancient history. Something best left in the past. "Pull it together. Don't let him know how you feel," she muttered, tugging off her top. "Keep your mouth closed, and he'll be gone in the morning."

***

In the corner of the couch, Lauren sat dressed in a pair of pink fleece pajama bottoms and an oversized white sweatshirt with ballet slippers and the name of a dance school on the front. She'd pulled her hair up in a ponytail and washed her makeup off. The sight of her like that threw him back fifteen years. How many times back then had they sat with her dressed in a similar manner watching television or studying?

He tried not to think about all those occasions and how they'd usually ended with them wrapped in each other's arms. Instead, he continued his search for something to watch and flipped to the next channel. So far the power had remained on, although it had flickered a few times. When a pass through all the channels failed to catch his attention, he went back to the twenty-four-hour news channel but hit the mute button. Should he attempt a conversation? They'd shared some small talk over dinner but nothing of consequence. And since her trip into her bedroom, she'd remained silent.

"Do you teach dance there?" He pointed to her sweatshirt.

Lauren's head shot up from the magazine in her hands, and then she glanced down at her sweatshirt. "Two nights a week during the school year."

"Ballet?" She had done all kinds of dance when he'd known her, but ballet had been her favorite.

Her brows creased in confusion.

"Don't you think I remember how much you liked ballet, Lauren?" Just because they'd been apart didn't mean he'd forgotten her likes and dislikes. At one time their lives had been so entwined they'd known every single detail about each other.

Lauren looked away. "It's been a long time, Nate."

"Some things you never forget. We both know that."

Her head snapped back around, a challenge in her eyes. "And some things we forget very easily." An undercurrent of anger laced her tone.

Nate held her gaze. "Care to explain?"

"There's nothing to explain. Not now anyway." For the first time all evening her polite tone dropped away. "Let's just leave it and watch TV."

Leave it? After her implication, he couldn't just

leave it. "Not happening. What did you mean?" Even if the best he could ever hope for was her friendship, he needed to get past her anger first.

Lauren unexpectedly jumped to her feet, took a few steps away, and whirled around to face him. "Fine. You want to talk about the past? We'll talk. You promised to write. Do you remember that, too?" She took a step closer. "That day you said we'd stay in contact, but you never bothered."

His gut winced. When he'd said the words way back then he'd meant them. He'd even tried once. He had picked up the phone, started to dial, and hung up. Just like then, Nate was unsure of what he intended to say now as he stood and began, "Lauren let me—"

"Don't make up any excuses." She stepped toward him and jabbed a finger into his shoulder. "I don't want to hear it. Besides, it doesn't matter now. We've both moved on."

In one motion, Nate wrapped his hand around her wrist and pulled her closer. The sudden physical contact caused his heart rate to rev like the engine of his brother's prized Corvette. "Bullshit."

With his hand still wrapped around her wrist, she took a step away from him. "Soon you'll go back to wherever the military wants you. We may never see each other again. The past doesn't matter."

"Like I told you the other night, Lauren. I am not leaving." He focused on removing the anger from his voice.

A cynical smile formed on her face. "You left the Marines? Yeah, right. They mean more to you than I ever did." The anger he'd heard before diminished, but sadness took its place.

Nate reached out his free hand and touched her cheek. "That's not true, and I'm no longer on active duty." The warmth from her skin managed to penetrate through the calluses on his hands. "I'm in the reserves now. Last month I graduated from the FBI Academy in Quantico."

Lauren's eyes flew open. "You're an FBI Agent? Seriously?" Her voice hit the next octave.

Surprise and shock trumped anger any day of the week. "Yeah, in the Boston field office."

"Wow, that's . . ." The awe in her voice trailed off. "That doesn't change anything." She took a step back, and his hand fell away.

With the increased distance between them again, the sunshine he'd felt bathed in a moment ago disappeared. "I don't believe that." In two steps he closed the distance between them. Before she could move again he made his move. He let his lips brush against hers.

Home. The word lit up in his head. Regardless of the years gone by, he belonged right here with this woman. He always had.

All messages between her brain and muscles stopped. For that brief moment she could only relish the feel of his firm lips once again against hers after all this time. Then the paralysis wore off, and she placed both hands on his chest and shoved him hard. "That didn't happen."

Nate folded his arms across his chest. "Yeah, Lauren, it did."

Her eyes traveled down his face to his arms where his biceps strained against his shirtsleeves. Back in high school he'd been fit and muscular, but the years since then had taken his unrefined body and sculpted it to perfection.

Don't get distracted. "I'm seeing Kevin."

He took a step closer. Despite the warning bells in her head, a flash of heat and excitement burst through her body.

"Simple. Stop seeing him."

The rich timber of Nate's voice washed over her, triggering both desire and annoyance at the same time. Lauren latched onto the annoyance. "Kevin makes me happy." *It's not a lie.* He may not set her on fire, but they had fun together, and she felt safe with him. "Just because you're back changes nothing. I have a life, Nate. I didn't just sit around while you did your part saving the world."

Nate unfolded his arms then reached for her hand. "Lauren, give me a chance to explain. I—"

Rough calluses rubbed against her hand, a reminder of the different lives they had led since high school. "Nate, I'm glad you're home safe, but our relationship ended a long time ago. Maybe we can be friends again. That's it, though." Her last sentence came out almost as a whisper. If he'd come back into her life years ago, maybe her response would've been different. Now, though, too much time had passed.

Nate's jaw clenched, the only outward sign he felt

anything. No big surprise there. Even as children he had been great at hiding his emotions. "I need some air."

He disappeared out the front door onto the porch without his jacket. *Ah, the wonderful Nathaniel Callahan avoidance.* How many times had she seen that over the years? Oh well, at least it brought an end to their conversation.

Chapter 4

Lauren bolted upright in bed. Next to her, JoJo lifted her head as if to say *you woke me*. Then she heard it again. A gut-wrenching moan that sent a chill through her body.

Nate. In one movement she kicked off the covers and flicked on the bedside lamp. "Damn," she said when the light didn't turn on. Moonlight from outside provided just enough light to cross the room without banging into anything and grab the flashlight from her bureau. Another moan came from across the hall. Without hesitation, Lauren left the room. The light from the flashlight bounced off the closed bedroom door. Through it she heard Nate say something, but all she caught was the word "no."

"Nate?" His only response was another agony-filled moan. Lauren opened the door as Nate once again said, "No," his voice thick with grief. The bright beam from her LED flashlight washed over him. He'd stripped down to his underwear and his legs were twisted up in the bed sheets. Even though his eyes remained closed, his face was contorted in pain and his entire body gleamed with sweat. As she stood in the doorway, he moaned again, his head thrashing back and forth.

"Nate," she called again as she moved to the side of the bed. When no response came, she put down the flashlight and reached for his shoulders. "Wake up, Nate." She tried to give him a little shake but it was a bit like trying to move a cement slab. "Come on, Nate. Wake up." This time she raised her voice.

His eyes popped open, darted wildly around the room, and then locked on her face. Still unfocused, he stared at her, but she got the sense that although his eyes were on her, he wasn't really seeing her.

"Are you okay?" Now that he'd stopped moaning, she became aware of the warm slick skin under her hands and the oddly shaped scar she could feel on his left shoulder.

He blinked a few times. "Lauren?" His eyes moved around the room illuminated only by the flashlight then returned to her. Recognition finally filled his face.

"You were . . . dreaming." The pain and grief she saw on his face made her chest ache. Before she could do something stupid like hug him, she lifted her hands and clasped them together in her lap. "Are you okay?"

she asked again.

The mattress on the bed shifted underneath her as Nate pulled himself up. "Sorry I woke you." He raked his hand across his face. "I'm fine. It was just a dream."

Yeah, right. She may not have been an expert on the brain and how it behaved during sleep, but she knew people didn't normally moan and break out in a sweat when they slept. "That wasn't a dream, Nate." She unclasped her hands and placed a palm on his cheek. "Do you want to talk about it?" The stubble growing on his face scratched her fingers as she caressed his cheek.

His hand wrapped around her wrist holding her hand still. "I said I'm fine. It was just a dream I have sometimes. No big deal."

Evidently his definition of a big deal varied greatly from hers. Her common sense said to let it go. Her soul said something else. "If you need anything, I'm here." She'd loved him too much at one time to see him suffering now.

"I'm fine," he said again, the hard edge from his voice gone now.

Now is a good time to go. Lauren swallowed, comprehension hitting her full on. Nate sat virtually naked just inches away. Thanks to her extra bright flashlight she saw every bare inch of him in magnificent detail. Despite the little voice telling her otherwise, Lauren let her gaze roam from his face across his shoulders and chest and down his torso. Not an extra ounce of flesh existed on him. Reversing the track her eyes had just taken, she spotted the Marine insignia tattoo—the eagle, anchor, and globe—on his upper right bicep near his shoulder. Back in high school she never would've guessed he'd get a tattoo, yet it looked good on him. Almost natural, if that was possible.

"Thanks." Nate's voice washed over her, tugging her back to reality. His hand moved down her arm creating goosebumps on her skin.

Lauren met his hazel-blue eyes, unable to look away. For a moment it felt as if the clock had turned back fifteen years. As if drawn by a pulley, she leaned forward intent on one thing, kissing him again. A sudden shift on the mattress when JoJo leaped on the bed broke whatever spell she'd fallen under. With a jerk, Lauren pulled her arm away and jumped up. Unable to look at him again, Lauren focused on the wall behind him. "The power went out. There is a flashlight in the bureau if you need it." She sensed that he wanted to say something, so she didn't give him the opportunity. "I'm going back to bed. See you in the morning." Lauren took a few steps toward the door, but when JoJo didn't follow she stopped. "Come on, JoJo. Bed." The dog looked up in response to her name, but she didn't get off the bed. Instead she settled her head on her paws. Prepared to pull the dog off the bed, she moved toward her. "Come on, you silly goose. He doesn't want you to sleep in here tonight."

"She can stay if she wants."

Lauren's hand paused above the dog's collar. "Are you sure? She likes to hog the bed."

"Positive. Leave her."

Don't argue. Leave while you still can. After she gave JoJo one final pat, she retreated back to her own room and away from the temptation that Nate presented.

***

With one hand she covered a yawn while the other poured an extra-large mug of coffee. After the restless sleep she'd had, she needed all the caffeine she could get. Thank goodness the power was back on. Before doing anything else, she took a long swallow of the French-vanilla coffee. Combined with a splash of milk and two sugars, it was the perfect mix of sweet and creamy. The warm liquid washed through her body, warming her as well. While the power had come back on a good fifteen minutes earlier, the house still remained on the chilly side. It would probably take another hour or so before it reached her preferred temperature.

After a few more sips she moved on, prepared to tackle breakfast. The weekends were the only time she put extra effort into cooking breakfast. During the week she opted for things like cereal with fruit or yogurt mixed with granola. On Saturdays and Sundays though, she didn't need to rush, so French toast or homemade waffles often made the menu.

So far she'd heard nothing from the spare bedroom. In case that meant Nate still slept, she tried to be quiet as she moved around the kitchen. After living alone for so long, she'd gotten used to not worrying about waking someone else up. Even if she didn't wake him, at some point he'd make an appearance. Then what? Should she bring up the scene last night or let it go? He'd brushed the dream off as nothing. The expression on his face said otherwise. Granted, people experienced nightmares all the time, yet a tiny voice said the dream he had last night was much more and something that happened often.

It's none of my business. Lauren cracked a few eggs into a bowl and then added some vanilla and milk. Nate had family and friends to talk to. He didn't need her interference. Besides, if she tried to help he may interpret it in the wrong way. Right now she didn't need that complication. Things with Kevin were going well. Too much interaction with Nate could jeopardize that relationship. With more force than necessary, Lauren beat the eggs together with the vanilla and milk before adding sugar and cinnamon to the mixture. Once satisfied, she set the bowl aside, dug out her skillet, and turned on the stove. All the while though, she kept an ear tuned for any movement in the spare bedroom. If he didn't wake up on his own soon, JoJo was sure to wake him. JoJo always woke her on the weekends when her bladder could wait no longer.

Nate felt the last remnants of sleep drift away. With reluctance, he opened his eyes. An unfamiliar room surrounded him, and a black dog slept with its head resting on the other pillow. Instantly his brain kicked in. Memories from the day before flashed through his head. *Lauren's house.* In one motion he swung his legs over the side of the bed and stood. Without even bothering to grab his jeans, he moved to the window. A winter wonderland greeted him. Snow no longer fell, but at least a foot of the white stuff covered the backyard. If he hoped to leave anytime soon he had some shoveling to do. Despite knowing what he needed to do, he stood at the window. It had been a while since he'd seen snow like this. If the temperature stayed as cold as it had been, this snow would be around past April Fool's Day.

Enough watching the scenery. Get your ass moving. Turning back toward the bed, Nate snatched up his jeans. Once dressed, he still held back. Sounds from the kitchen told him Lauren was up. He'd faced down enemies with weapons, yet a deep unease made him reluctant to face her this morning. Shame burned a hole in his chest, a bit like a flame burning its way through paper. No one knew about his nightmares. They'd started more than a year ago. Some weeks they came every night. Other times he'd go weeks between them. Every time they came he handled them in the same way. He'd stuff all the emotions they evoked back into the little box where they belonged and consider himself damn lucky. So many of his buddies suffered in ways much worse than dreams. If he had to deal with a few dreams every once in a while, he wouldn't complain.

The scene from last night wasn't the only thing that kept him in the bedroom. He'd kissed her. Something he had no right doing. Even though she had kissed him back, he had made the first move last night, which put all the blame on his shoulders. *Can't undo it, so get your ass out there.* If he could change the past, the kiss from the night before wouldn't be the only thing he'd undo.

"Come on, JoJo. Time to get out of bed." Nate rubbed the dog's head. At the sound of her name, the dog stretched out all four legs then jumped to the floor.

The scent of brewed coffee and breakfast pulled him down the short hallway into the kitchen. When he walked in, Lauren stood at the stove. Her long hair remained pulled back in a haphazard braid, and she wore pink fleece pants and a cotton top. She looked comfortable and relaxed as she worked. Even though he'd stopped to admire the view, JoJo darted past him. The dog sat down beside Lauren and looked up at her.

"I bet you want to go out," Lauren said as she put down the spatula in her hand.

"I'll let her out." Nate crossed the kitchen and opened the sliding glass door that led to the backyard. The dog didn't pause. She bounded down the stairs and across the snow-covered yard. Nate watched the dog run through the snow then turned away from the door. "Where do you keep the shovel?"

Lauren looked up from the stove. "Don't worry about it. A plow comes for the driveway." She didn't hold his gaze for long before turning her attention back to the food in the pan. "Breakfast is just about ready, anyway. Help yourself to some coffee. The mugs are in the corner cabinet."

An argument about shoveling could wait. He was

hungry, and from here it looked like she'd made French toast, his favorite breakfast food. "You need a refill?" Nate held up the coffee pot.

"I'm good for now. Have a seat." Lauren gestured toward a bar stool with the hand holding the plate piled high with food. The hint of cinnamon apples drifted toward him, and his mouth watered. "Don't wait for me. Start eating."

Before sitting, Nate let the dog back in. Snow clung to her face, especially around the muzzle. "Looks like someone likes the snow."

Lauren laughed, and the sound eased the tension in his chest. "JoJo's a bit of snow bunny," she said.

Nate took another sip of his coffee. For now, he'd wait and let her pick a topic of conversation. Last night he'd tried and had ended up arguing with her. He didn't want to argue with Lauren. "This looks great. Thanks." He picked up his fork with a small smile on his face. His plate was piled high with French toast covered with caramelized apples, just the way he liked it. He'd bet that she'd added cinnamon and nutmeg to the French toast, too. Nate took his first bite. The combination of flavors exploded in his mouth and sent his mind reeling back to all the times his mother had made French toast just like this. Living next door, Lauren would often stop over in the morning on the weekends and join them. She always complained that her mom thought the only breakfast foods in the world either came from a cereal box or fit inside a toaster.

Taking the seat next to him, Lauren started on her own breakfast, French toast minus the apples. Instead she had added a few raspberries on top. "Did you sleep okay last night?"

It was a valid question. One anyone would ask someone who had spent the night. Nate sensed by her tone that she was asking more than her words implied. "Great." He shoveled another forkful of food into his mouth. It wasn't a lie. With the exception of his nightmare, he had slept well. The unexpected warmth of her hand on his arm caused him to bite his tongue as he chewed. Still, the quick stab of pain didn't affect the heat building in his body.

"If you . . . um . . . ever want to talk or anything, Nate, I'm here." Her voice resonated with compassion and concern.

Nate bit back a curse, then worrying she'd pull her hand away, he covered it with his own, anchoring her to him. "Nothing to talk about unless you mean us."

"I saw you last night. That was no normal dream you had."

If she wanted to ignore the past between them for now, fine, but he wasn't talking about his nightmares either. "Let it go, Lauren. Everyone gets nightmares. It's no big deal."

"Nate—" Lauren's voice took on a pleading tone.

"Lauren, I'm fine," he snapped. "Let's just finish eating." Removing his hand, he picked up his fork. Irritation made him stab his food as if it might grow legs and run away. Her insistence that he open up indicated she still cared. He should have been pleased about that. All he felt, though, was embarrassment.

After his suggestion, Lauren pulled her hand away and remained silent as she ate her own food. The longer the silence remained, the more Nate wanted to kick himself for being such an ass. She meant well and he shouldn't have snapped at her. *Time to apologize.* "Lauren, I'm sorry, but I am fine."

Lauren gave him a stiff nod in acknowledgment without even looking in his direction.

"Did Kelly have the baby last night?" Maybe a conversation about the newest member of her family would put her in a better mood.

Lauren's hand paused with her coffee mug raised almost to her mouth. "She sent me a text message around three o'clock. She and the baby are fine. Jared almost passed out during the delivery, but he's okay, too."

He waited for her to add more. When she remained silent again, he prompted her with another question. "Did she have a boy or girl?"

"A little girl. They named her Beth." Lauren smiled. "Kelly sent a picture too." Lauren grabbed her cell phone. "Can you believe all the hair she has?"

Nate accepted the phone Lauren held out to him, glad that at least for the moment she had forgotten she was upset with him.

"I think she looks just like Kelly," she said.

He squinted at the tiny picture on the screen. The baby did have a ton of hair. Granted, he hadn't spent much time around babies, but he'd expected her to be nearly bald, not have enough hair to comb. As far as looking like Lauren's sister, well, if she said so, he damn well wasn't going to disagree. From the picture, the only hint the baby was female was the pink blanket wrapped around her. "Congratulations, Auntie."

She beamed at him as she took the phone back.

Stabbing the last piece of French toast with his fork, Nate popped it into his mouth. With Lauren in a good mood now, perhaps he should head out and start shoveling before he managed to put his foot in his mouth again. "Thanks for breakfast. I'm going to start on the outside now." He didn't wait for response.

Once outside, he could breathe again. Inside the kitchen with Lauren right next to him, his body had been on sensory overload. Everything from the way she looked to the sound of her voice caused every cell in his brain to shout *mine*. His arms ached to hold her again the way he had the night before. To taste her lips. But while his body demanded he reach for her, his brain told him to back off. She was with someone else, and he needed to respect that. Unfortunately, it was the last thing he wanted to do.

Perhaps the worst part of it all was that he knew she cared. All the signs were there. The framed photo, the effort she put into preparing foods he liked. If she really felt nothing, she could have just as easily given him a plain grilled cheese last night and cereal this morning. Then, of course, there was her reaction to his nightmare.

Digging the shovel into the snow, he scooped up another load of the white stuff and tossed it away from the front steps. He hated that she had seen him like that. Even now in the light of day, he could picture the worry and compassion on her face. Not to mention her touch. The feel of her hand on his bare skin after so many years had sent all his blood south. And even with the remnants of his nightmare fresh in his mind, he wanted to lay her down and show her how much he loved her.

With his body still aroused, thanks to Lauren, he was half-tempted to strip down and dive into the snow. What would her neighbors say about that? If nothing else, it would give the whole town something to talk about for several days. Small towns were all like that. They loved to gossip.

Finished with the stairs, Nate started on the walkway. The snow was light and fluffy, allowing him to put little effort into the task, despite the amount that had accumulated overnight.

Over the years he'd developed a sixth sense when it came to being observed—something that came in handy in a war zone. And right now he knew he was being watched. Dropping the end of the shovel into the snow, he looked up. Lauren stood at the large bay window, a mug in her hand and her eyes glued to him. When their eyes met, she held his gaze for a few seconds, her forehead creased, and then she walked away.

Lifting up more snow, he blew out a breath. Why did this have to be so damn difficult? Why wouldn't she let him explain why he'd made the decisions he did all those years ago? Why couldn't she just admit she still cared and tell him what it would take to win her back? It was clear, though, she didn't plan to do any of that. So where did that leave him? Alone and hoping that in time she'd change her mind.

When he went out and started on the steps, she remained silent. After snowstorms she always cleared the steps and walkway, she could handle that much, while a local landscaper came by and plowed the driveway. But the landscaper usually took care of his clients closer to his house before making it to her side of town. So, if Nate insisted on clearing the snow this morning, she'd let him. If nothing else, it would get him out of here sooner. And the one thing she needed this morning, more than anything, was Nate out of her house. She'd underestimated how difficult it would be having him in her house all night and again in the morning when she got up. But then again, even if she had known, she would have asked him to stay. If she'd let him leave the night before in the thick of the storm and something had happened to him she never would have forgiven herself. As much as she might try to deny it, she cared. She cared far more than she should, considering she was dating someone else.

With her coffee mug in hand, she moved toward the window. Outside, he removed the snow as if it weighed nothing at all. When she shoveled, she always ended up sore and tired. Shoveling snow used muscles in ways that dancing did not. But Nate made it look effortless.

He'd always been strong, but thanks to her visit to his room last night, she knew firsthand just how much muscle he'd put on. Warmth spread through her limbs at the memory of him half-naked in bed. *No, no, no. I'm with Kevin. Think of him instead.* She squeezed her eyes closed. Instead of an image of Kevin, however, another memory of Nate formed.

She hadn't seen his kiss coming. One minute he told her he worked for the FBI and the next she found herself wrapped in his arms, his lips against hers. In the deepest recess of her mind, she'd known it was wrong the minute he made contact. Even so, she'd let herself enjoy the moment. No one other than Nate had ever been able to kick-start her desire with a simple kiss. And once again the night before he had done just that. For the tiniest of moments she'd considered forgetting about the past for one night and experiencing the magic she'd only ever known with him. Just as quickly, though, she remembered all the reasons she could not let that happen. And when he acted as if a simple kiss could fix fifteen years of separation, her blood pressure had skyrocketed. Last night she'd told him that the only thing that could ever exist between them was friendship. But could they even have that? Every time she saw him, her heart ached. For her own sanity, it would be better if they stayed away from each other altogether. But after last night, the thought of not seeing him made her want to cry.

Nate's eyes locked with hers from the other side of the window. She held his gaze as long as she dared and then turned away. *Great way to show you're not interested.* If she had any hope of convincing Nate, she'd better start convincing herself first.

Chapter 5

Lauren double-checked her reflection in the full-length mirror. The gown Callie gave her as a birthday present fit her as if it had been custom made for her. Taking a step back, she smoothed out any visible wrinkles, the fabric sleek and rich between her fingers. Never in a million years had she pictured herself owning a Dolce & Gabbana gown. And if not for Callie, she wouldn't. Part of her felt a little guilty. While Callie and her husband could afford such extravagant gifts without even batting an eyelash, Lauren knew there was no way she could ever give Callie anything even remotely as expensive. The gown, as beautiful as it was, was just another reminder of how much her life and Callie's were different now.

"Well, JoJo, tonight's the night. Finally, I get to meet the elusive parents." Lauren stepped away from the mirror as she talked to the dog lounging on the bed. Her stomach did a somersault at the thought. Kevin had invited her to a dinner party at his parents' estate in Weston. Since he rarely spoke about them when together, she knew very little about his parents. She knew his dad had been the CEO of the family's company, Walsh and Miles Construction, the largest construction company on the East Coast, until Kevin took his place. Thanks to the Internet, she knew Kevin's grandfather had started Walsh Construction right around the end of World War II. She also knew Kevin's father had expanded the business when he married Kevin's mother, Sherry Miles, and acquired Miles Construction. Hopefully, tonight she'd learn more than what she could find on the web.

On the bed, JoJo remained still, only coming to life when the doorbell rang. Then she took off for the front door like a Kentucky Derby racehorse with Lauren trailing behind.

"Wow! You look gorgeous," Kevin said before dropping a kiss on her cheek.

Lauren smiled as she closed the front door and did a quick once over of Kevin. As always he was dressed impeccably. Tonight he wore a dark navy blue tailor-made suit and looked just as handsome as ever. Despite all that, Lauren felt only a minor pull of attraction when he smiled at her. Not even a tiny thread of excitement ran through her body. *We're still getting to know each other.* Once again, Lauren reminded herself it was still early in their relationship. *Give it time.*

"If you're ready, we should go." He moved closer to Lauren but stopped when JoJo inserted her body between them, all the while barking. Immediately, Kevin backed away. "Your dog really doesn't like people, does she?" he asked, brushing a few dog hairs from his pants.

Lauren grabbed onto JoJo's collar and tugged her toward the kitchen. "I've never seen her act like this before." Since the day she'd brought the dog home, JoJo had been friendly, the type of animal who loved attention and who liked cuddling up next to you on the couch. Sure, she barked when a stranger came to the door, but once Lauren made it clear the stranger was welcome, she backed off. Yet so far, the dog hadn't warmed up to Kevin at all. Lauren assumed it was because he all but ignored her whenever he came to the house. Still, she had never carried on like she did tonight. "I'll put her in the kitchen and we can go."

During the hour-long ride from Lauren's house to the Walsh's estate in Weston they discussed everything from Lauren's new niece to Kevin's week at work. While the conversation covered a lot of territory, the topics remained superficial. Lauren never once got into the details about the day her niece was born or even if she'd come home from the hospital yet. Kevin didn't seem to mind. While others might ask about the baby's size or other such details, he'd been satisfied with the news that Kelly had had the baby, and Lauren didn't offer any additional information.

Especially the part when Nate came across her broken-down car and ended up spending the night, thanks to the snowstorm. An iota of guilt nagged at her for not telling Kevin about Nate, but another part insisted she not worry about it. After all, nothing had happened. Well, almost nothing. He had kissed her, but it only happened that once. And afterward she'd made it clear she wasn't interested—or at least she tried. Nate's tone that night made it sound as if he didn't care if she was dating someone or not.

I'm not letting him back in. Once she had put all her love and trust in him and he'd up and walked out on her. Never again would she set herself up for that. Not even for Nate. So, since she planned on keeping Nathaniel Callahan at a distance, Kevin never needed to know he'd spent the night in her spare bedroom.

"You said you had a surprise." Kevin's voice invaded her thoughts.

Looking away from the window, she studied Kevin's profile. What was wrong with her, anyway? She was out with a handsome, very successful executive, and she was thinking about an old high school love. So many women she knew would give anything to be right where she was now. *Get your head back on straight.*

"Callie gave me tickets for the ballet and hotel reservations for a weekend in New York City as a birthday present. It's in two weeks. I thought we could go together." She'd gone back and forth about inviting Kevin. They hadn't known each other long. Maybe it was too soon for a whole weekend together in New

York. But she wanted to share the experience with someone, and Kevin seemed like the logical choice.

Thanks to the streetlights, Lauren saw the curt nod he gave her before turning into a driveway. Kevin stopped in front of the iron gate, punched in a security code, and the gate swung open. "Remind me later, and I'll save it on my calendar."

Lauren smiled as Kevin drove down the winding driveway. On some level she'd feared he would say something like *we'll see* or *I'll try*. During the time they'd been dating, Kevin's calendar appeared to fill up months in advance. The ballet was right around the corner, so that didn't give him much notice.

"Is this a big party tonight?"

Kevin brought the car around one final turn and a huge Tudor-style mansion aglow with light came into view. With ease, Kevin pulled up behind another car. "For my parents, tonight's dinner is small."

While an answer, it didn't provide Lauren with much information.

The overhead light in the car came on when Kevin opened his door."My parents are looking forward to meeting you tonight."

Before she could offer any response, he got out and started around to her side of the car. Lauren focused on the large water fountain in front of the mansion, her stomach up somewhere in her throat much like it had been the first and only time she'd tried skydiving. She wanted this. For weeks now, she had stewed about not meeting any of Kevin's family while he'd met much of hers.

Lauren shivered when the car door opened. The gown Callie gave her might be gorgeous, but it definitely wasn't warm enough for this cold night.

"Let's get you inside where it is warm." Kevin offered his hand.

Kevin's parents were more or less just what she had expected: impeccably dressed, well groomed, and aloof. They said all the right words, asked all the right questions, but she could tell they were not hearing any of her responses. Although, she could never explain how she knew that. Of course, behavior similar to theirs was not uncommon. She had met many socialites at Callie's parties who shared the same tendency—and not just with outsiders like her but within their own circles. Thankfully, she'd also met some who did not exhibit this habit. Or at least if they did, they were much better at pretending to be interested.

Tonight Lauren tried not to let Kevin's parents' behavior bother her as she watched them interact with the other guests. His dad acted that way to everyone present, including his wife. So far she hadn't seen the two of them converse with each other. Kevin's mom spent most of her time with the governor's wife. Despite Lauren's effort to ignore it, their behavior did bother her. This was the first time she had met them. She'd thought his parents would want get to know the woman their son was dating. At least, that was how things worked in her family. From the looks of it, Mr. and Mrs. Walsh had other priorities.

"Kevin said you teach elementary school." Olivia,

Kevin's sister, sat next to her at the dinner table. Olivia was an attractive young woman, but Lauren never would have guessed she and Kevin were sister and brother. While Kevin had dark chestnut hair and brown eyes, his sister was the complete opposite with the blondest hair she had ever seen and a porcelain complexion that probably burned rather than tanned in the summer. The only family characteristic the siblings shared was their height. Olivia stood almost as tall as her six foot brother and father .

Lauren nodded. "Fifth grade. I taught second for a few years, but found I liked working with the older students more." She'd always thought she wanted to do early childhood education. She even did her student teaching in a first grade classroom. Then after two years as a second grade teacher, the principal moved her up to the fifth grade when they needed to shuffle teachers around due to class size. Initially, she had dreaded the change. Now after nine years, she could not imagine teaching any other age group.

"And you actually like it?"

To someone who had probably never stepped foot in a public school classroom, she guessed it might seem odd that she loved her job so much. "I do. Sometimes it drives me a little crazy, but overall I can't imagine doing anything else."

Olivia gave her a you-poor-thing smile and then reached for her fork.

Lauren eyed her own plate and what she suspected were snails. In some parts of the world they may be considered a delicacy, but she could not bring herself to try them. So rather than reach for her fork, she kept on talking and hoped no one noticed she wasn't eating.

"I also teach ballet at a dance school in town."

"Really? I adore the ballet. My absolute favorite is *Swan Lake*. I've lost count of how many times I have seen it performed."

"It is wonderful. I saw it performed in Boston last year. But I think my favorite is *Coppelia*. It was the first ballet I saw performed on stage."

"My first ballet was *Cinderella*. My mom took me, and I kept waiting for the Fairy Godmother to turn a pumpkin into a carriage. At the time the Disney movie was my favorite, and I watched it all the time. When no actual pumpkin magically changed, I cried."

His parents had said tonight's dinner would be an intimate affair, and for his parents this meant four other couples, not counting themselves. He'd hoped for a few less guests. Lauren always came across as outgoing and confident, but still, he wanted her first encounter with his family to be smooth and comfortable. While Lauren may socialize with the Sherbrookes and Talbots, she really wasn't a part of that society. For the most part, she existed within the middle class. While there was nothing wrong with that, what was considered acceptable there may or may not be proper with the likes of his parents.

Under the table Kevin rested his hand on Lauren's thigh and gave a little squeeze. Next to him, she continued her debate with his sister as to which ballet was better, *Giselle* or *Swan Lake,* but her hand slipped under the table and rested on his. Her action spoke volumes. Sometimes he found it difficult to gauge Lauren's feelings and just how invested she was in their relationship. Tonight though, her words and actions told him a lot. Inwardly he smiled, interlaced his fingers with hers, and turned his complete attention to the conversation he'd started with his father and Barry Clarkson. Any remaining reservations he'd entertained since her mother's retirement party disappeared.

***

"So what else do you know about her?" Clinton Walsh asked.

With dinner over, Kevin and his father had retreated to his father's office for a private conversation while the rest of the guests socialized over after-dinner drinks. Kevin rested his ankle on his knee and made himself comfortable in the armchair. On the other side of the wide desk, his father sat with a brandy in his hand.

"Her mother just retired, and her father teaches at Adams Hall. Lauren graduated from there."

"What about the rest of her family? Brothers, sisters? What do you know about them?"

Kevin lifted his own brandy toward his mouth. "Don't you think I would've checked into all this beforehand? There are no black sheep in her family."

Clinton's fingers drummed on the desk. "I'm still

not convinced. She is only a schoolteacher."

Don't let him get to you. Kevin took a minute before answering. "Lauren is a well-educated woman, and I enjoy spending time with her. We share enough of the same interests and values to make a relationship work. I'm confident she'll agree." The one thing he knew better than business was women, and he could read Lauren like an open book. She missed her best friend, Callie Talbot. She went to visit Callie and her new world, but she didn't really belong. He could help with that. While he may not be quite as wealthy as Callie's husband, his wealth allowed him to travel in many of the same social circles. His wealth would also allow Lauren to pursue her dreams in earnest. She had told him how much she wanted to travel and how she wanted to open her own dance studio rather than simply teach part-time at a school owned by someone else. He could give her all those things and much more.

"When will you ask her?"

Kevin swallowed the last of his brandy. "I haven't decided, but soon." Since the retirement party and Lauren's run-in with her former neighbor, he'd felt an urgency to keep their relationship moving forward. Even though she'd tried to play it cool, something about her mannerisms that night gave her away. She might want everyone to think she had no feelings for the guy, but Kevin suspected the two of them had a deep history. A history that remained unresolved, and it wasn't only that night. Since the party, their phone conversations had changed, too.

"Good luck, then." Clinton came to his feet. "Let me know how it goes."

Once again, Lauren glanced over Olivia's shoulder toward the doorway. Since Kevin's sister continued speaking without so much as a pause, Lauren assumed she had not noticed. Although she found Olivia's description of the fashions she'd seen at a recent Hollywood party interesting, Lauren wanted Kevin to walk through the doorway now. Being in a room full of strangers had never bothered her, yet tonight she wished she owned an invisibility cloak.

"And to say the designs by Marcella Horton were beautiful is an understatement. Photos just don't do them justice," Olivia said, referring to the newest designer to hit it big with the A-list celebrities in Hollywood.

Lauren nodded because it seemed like the thing to do. "I saw a picture of the gown she designed for Mia Troy. It was amazing."

At the mention of the popular film actress, Olivia launched into details of the conversation she'd had with the woman during her last trip to California. Lauren once again fell silent, allowing Olivia to dominate the conversation, which in this instance she was okay with. Shifting in her chair, Lauren readjusted the hem of her dress once again, thankful Callie had given her such a present. While a layer of guilt remained because she could never give Callie a gift even half as expensive, she loved the way it looked on her, and it was perfect for this evening's dinner party.

Both Kevin's mom and sister had complimented her on it. It also helped her fit in much better tonight. All the women at the dinner party wore gowns by some of the top designers. Granted, when she saw Callie or any of Callie's family she never thought about the labels on her clothes, yet around Kevin's family they stayed in the forefront of her mind, even though the Walshes didn't possess the power and wealth the Sherbrookes and Talbots did.

"Kevin mentioned that you and Callie Talbot are close friends." Olivia's new topic grabbed Lauren's full attention.

"We've known each other a long time. We even taught together before she married." How she missed those days. Michelle, the teacher in Callie's old classroom, was nice, but this was her first year with her own classroom. Often, rather than working as a team like they were supposed to, Lauren acted as more of a mentor, which she didn't mind except that wasn't her job. Tonya, the teacher across the hall who planned to teach for only another year, was supposed to be Michelle's mentor.

"Have you met her brother Jake?" Olivia looked over toward her husband and then leaned a little closer. "Is he as hot in person as he is in pictures? I don't care if I am married, if he ever asked me to sleep with him, I would in a heartbeat."

Lauren cleared her throat in an attempt to cover her surprise. "I've met him several times." Okay, so several was putting it mildly. She'd seen him at many Sherbrooke events Callie had invited her to, as well as at Callie and Dylan's place in New York countless times when she'd gone to visit.

"I keep waiting to read he's getting a divorce. It's got to be just a matter of time. A man like him can't be faithful forever. At some point he'll be on the prowl for someone else, if he isn't already." Olivia spoke as if she was an authority on the matter.

Even though Jake Sherbrooke, Callie's half-brother, was happily married, it appeared his reputation still followed him. Too bad Olivia, like most people, had it all wrong about him. "I don't see that happening."

"Don't see what happening?" Kevin asked from behind her.

At the sound of his voice, Lauren turned around. Warmth crept up her cheeks. She didn't want Kevin to know they had been discussing another man. "I didn't see you come in," Lauren said, ignoring his question.

"I came in the other door." Kevin sat down next to her. "What don't you see happening?" he asked again.

Across from them Olivia waved a hand toward her brother. "Just talking about how successful a celebrity marriage will be. Nothing that would interest you."

Lauren gave Olivia what she hoped was a smile, and for the first time all night, she thought maybe she could somehow become friends with this woman. Like Kevin's parents and the other guests there, Olivia had been polite but not friendly. At least not until now.

"You and my sister seemed to get along well." Kevin gave her hand a squeeze as he drove. "She doesn't usually take to new people the way she did to you."

"Really? Maybe it was because we found something in common, the ballet."

"Olivia does love the ballet. She trained at The School of American Ballet in New York for years. Before my mother convinced her otherwise, she hoped to join the New York City Ballet."

Why would any parent convince their child not to strive for what she wanted? Especially if she had the talent to achieve that goal. If she ever had children, she would never stop them from pursuing what they truly wanted. "She must have been very good if that school admitted her. Why didn't your mom want her to continue?"

Kevin put both hands on the steering wheel, his eyes focused on the road. "Let's just say a ballerina would do little for Walsh and Miles."

His tone made Lauren wonder if he'd had other ambitions besides a career in business. She could not picture him as anything but a successful CEO, yet that meant nothing. Pressure from parents to pursue certain avenues in life was not unheard of. Her own parents had supported all the decisions she and her siblings made, but many of her classmates in high school had faced such pressure. If Kevin had bowed to his parents' pressure, would he expect the same from his own children? While way too soon in the relationship to be thinking about children, the answer to such a question would tell her a lot about him. Depending on how far this thing between them went, she'd have to approach the subject. But not tonight. Who knew how he might interpret such a question?

"What did she do instead?"

"She got a degree in finance. Olivia worked for the company until she married Greg last year."

She couldn't imagine the woman she'd spoken with at dinner being happy pouring over financial numbers and spreadsheets. "What about you? Did you ever think about doing something other than business?"

"When I was ten, I decided to be a rock star like the ones on TV. I already knew how to play the piano, so I took up the drums. Practiced every free minute for about three years. Gave it up when I went to boarding school. I haven't touched a drum set since."

When she'd asked the question, she hadn't been referring to his childhood dreams. Few people followed through with those. If they did, there would be an over-abundance of astronauts and doctors in the world. "What about later on?" They passed under a streetlight, and she noticed Kevin's grip on the steering wheel tighten.

"No, I planned to take over for my father and then venture into politics at some point."

"When I was ten I wanted to be an actress in the movies. Then for a while I wanted to be a dolphin trainer. Sometime around my junior year in high school I decided on teaching."

"I'm sure your parents were happy when you

decided against the dolphins."

"I don't think so. They always supported everything I wanted to try. Dance, singing, art classes. They did the same with Kelly and Matt. One summer they even let Matt go to space camp because he insisted he wanted to be an astronaut. What about you?"

"My parents made sure I had plenty of extracurricular activities," Kevin answered stiffly, before lapsing into silence for the remainder of the car ride.

Chapter 6

Nate pulled into a spot in the parking lot of O'Donnell's Family Restaurant and Pub. After a day of interviewing victims, he wanted nothing more than a cheeseburger and a cold beer. Both of which he could get here.

Passing by the door into the restaurant side, he headed straight into the pub. Despite the crowded parking lot, few patrons were inside. Two guys sat at the bar while two more played a game of pool down at the far end of the pub.

"Do you want a menu?" the bartender, a bodybuilder type with a bald head, asked when Nate sat down.

"No need. Give me a cheeseburger and a bottle of

Sam Adams."

The bartender slapped a cardboard coaster on the bar and nodded. "You got it."

Behind Nate the door opened, sending in a blast of unusually cool April air. Nate didn't bother to look over. Instead, he looked up at the large-screen TV hung on the wall where the sportscaster gave his predictions for that weekend's Bruins game against the Rangers. Out of the corner of his eye, he saw someone pull out a bar stool and sit.

"Callahan," a male voice said.

He immediately recognized the voice and turned to find Matthew McDonald, Lauren's older brother, seated next to him. "Hey, Matt. On your way home?"

When the bartender put a bottle of beer in front of each of them before Matt said a word, Nate assumed Matt was a regular at the pub.

"No. I come here every Thursday night. I'm in a pool league. Starts in another thirty minutes."

Nate took a swallow of his beer. Maybe he'd look into the league at some point. It'd be a good way to reconnect with the guys in town. Although, his job might make it difficult to commit. Most nights he got home by seven, but it wasn't a guarantee. A career with the FBI wasn't exactly a nine to five position.

"Lauren told me what happened the other night," Matt said with a hard edge to his voice.

The mention of Lauren's name caused Nate's mind to zero in on that night at her house. Waking up from his nightmares with her leaning over him had sent his body and mind swirling through emotions.

Everything from desire to shame assaulted him. That night had also told him something. Lauren still cared, despite her words of denial. She hadn't hesitated to come in when she thought he needed her, and she'd made his favorite breakfast.

Even with the hints that she cared, Lauren still refused to outright admit it, and so far he hadn't come up with a good way to melt the ice barrier she'd erected between them. So, rather than beat his head against it, he'd backed off.

Nate opened his mouth prepared to answer when the bartender placed his food in front of him. The scent of the grilled burger and melted cheese made his stomach rumble. He'd skipped lunch and right then he figured he could down two of these burgers. "There was no way I could leave her stranded out there. Only an asshole would do that." Even if it hadn't been Lauren stuck out there that night, he would have stopped and helped.

"We all know you're not that." Matt's voice dripped with sarcasm.

Nate's hand paused with the cheeseburger halfway to his mouth. "What's that supposed to mean?"

"You left her to fend for herself once before."

Using all his self-control, he brought the burger back down to the plate. He wasn't used to anyone talking to him with such animosity and disrespect. "What the hell are you talking about?" Nate rested his forearms on the bar, his hands clenched and his knuckles white.

Matt glared at him as he took a swig from his own beer bottle. "The summer you took off for the Naval Academy and left her to handle things herself."

Nothing Lauren's brother said made any sense. "If you've got something to say, then say it. Otherwise get lost." He didn't even try to keep his voice low. The guy was pissing him off.

Matt's face exploded with fury, and he slammed his beer bottle down on the bar. Around them people turned to look, and the bodybuilder bartender headed their way. "Forget did you? Let me refresh your memory. After you two graduated, you took off and left my sister behind pregnant. Real upstanding of you."

An IED exploded in Nate's chest and he stopped breathing. *Lauren pregnant? Baby?* No, Matt was wrong. She would've told him. "Bullshit." His voice came out strangled. "She never said anything." She would've told him something like that.

Matt shrugged a shoulder as some of the red faded from his face. "Maybe she thought you knew. Hell, even I suspected before she told me. She was so sick that summer. She couldn't eat anything, and she slept so much."

He did remember that, but back then he'd assumed it was stress and anxiety. Their lives were about to change as they left for college. "I didn't . . ." His voice trailed off as questions mounted. How could she have kept something like that from him? Where was the child now? Had she given it up for adoption? Had she had an abortion? Nate needed answers and he needed them now. Pulling a twenty out of his wallet, he dropped it next to his plate, which contained his uneaten meal. Without another glance at Matt, he stood.

"Leave her alone, Callahan. Lauren's happy and with someone. She doesn't need you messing up her life again."

Nate ignored Matt. As much as his fist wanted to make contact with Matt's face, he walked past Lauren's brother and out the door.

Somehow, he managed to make it from the pub to Lauren's without getting into an accident, although he didn't know how. Anger filled him as he drove, making it impossible to focus on anything. From her driveway he saw a light on inside the house. As he approached the front door he heard JoJo barking before he even rang the doorbell. Then as if he'd conjured her up, Lauren pulled open the door, a calm expression on her face.

How can she be so relaxed? Right then he felt like a ticking time bomb of emotion ready to explode. Without waiting for an invitation inside, he pushed past her then grabbed the door from her hand and slammed it closed. Perhaps sensing Nate's anger, JoJo stepped in front of Lauren as if to protect her.

"Nate, what's—" Lauren began taking a step away from him.

"Why the hell didn't you tell me?" Nate shouted in a harsh, raw voice.

"Listen, Nate, I don't know what you're talking about, but now isn't the time. I just got home from teaching ballet to six-year-old girls. I'm tired." Lauren crossed her arms over her chest, her voice defensive. "Whatever the problem is it'll have to wait."

For the first time he noticed her attire. She wore a pink leotard and gray sweatpants and her hair was tied up in a bun. Nate ignored her request, despite the evidence she'd just gotten home. She had kept this secret from him long enough. He needed the truth now.

"How could you keep that from me?" Nate advanced on her completely ruled by emotions rather than common sense. "I deserved to know you were pregnant with my child."

All the color drained from Lauren's face, and she swayed on her feet. "Who told you?" she whispered, her voice barely audible.

The urge to lash out at Lauren while at the same time comfort her collided in his head. Her shell-shocked expression pulled at his heart, but his anger at her silence kept him from embracing her. "Your brother, but you should have. Fifteen years ago, Lauren."

Lauren sank down onto the couch without saying another word. When she glanced up at him, her eyes glistened with unshed tears. "When you left for the Academy, I didn't know." Her voice quivered as she spoke. "I found out two weeks after you left. I planned on telling you when I heard from you." Tears fell down her face. "You promised to keep in touch even though we were no longer together. You said we would always be friends, remember?"

He heard the accusation in her voice. When he'd made the promise, he'd fully intended to keep it, but then after a while he figured it was better for both of them if he kept his distance. Let her get on with her life. At eighteen it had made plenty of sense. Now, at thirty-three, he realized what an ass he'd been.

"When you never called, I got the message loud and clear, Nate. You didn't care about me."

Nate paced back and forth several times in front of the couch, guilt eating away at his heart. "I had a right to know, Lauren. You should've told me. I would've—"

Lauren shot to her feet. "Would have what, Nate? Come home? Left the Academy?" She advanced on him, her eyes blazing with anger now. "You made it clear when you broke up with me that your military career meant more to you than I did."

Damn, he was close to losing control of the conversation. He hadn't come here to talk about his mistakes. He'd come for answers and so far he hadn't gotten any. "I broke up with you because I loved you. I didn't want you making all the sacrifices military families are forced to make. And I—"

She moved closer but stopped short of physically touching him. "We talked about that when you applied to Annapolis. You knew I would've stood by you no matter what. That was my decision to make, not yours."

Yeah, sure they'd discussed it before he'd applied, but that was before it became reality. Once it was a sure thing, he'd realized how much she'd have to give up if they stayed together while he served. At the time he made the decision to end their relationship because he honestly thought it would be best for both of them. Not that any of that mattered now. Right now he wanted to know about their child.

"If you had told me, I would have come home and taken care of both of you." For now he needed to stick with one topic at a time. "Was it a boy or a girl?" In his heart he knew Lauren never would've had an abortion and she obviously had no child living with her so she must have put the baby up for adoption.

The dam holding back Lauren's tears burst and sobs racked her body. On pure instinct he wrapped his arms around her and pulled her close. As she cried, he held her without saying a word. After a while Lauren's body stilled, and she became silent. As if realizing she stood embraced in his arms, she pulled back while at the same time she wiped the tears from her face with her hand.

"I don't know." Lauren looked at a spot on the wall behind him while she spoke. "I miscarried at twelve weeks."

His heart clenched with pain. "Lauren, I'm . . ." his voice trailed off. What should he say? True, it had happened a long time ago, but for him it was just happening. "What happened?"

She shrugged and met his eyes. "It's not uncommon for a woman to miscarry that early on. Some women don't even know they're pregnant at that point." More tears slid down her face, but her body no longer shook.

He knew very little about a woman's pregnancy past the creation phase, so he'd accept her word on that one. "I'm so . . . Lauren I wish . . ." He stopped, unsure of what he wanted to say. So instead of trying again, he moved closer and gathered her up in his arms. At first she remained still, but then she wrapped her arms around his waist and leaned into him.

"I wish you'd told me so I could have been here for you." Nate spoke softly. Anger still burned inside him, but so did loss. *A child*. They'd almost had a child together.

Lauren's arms tightened around him. "It's in the past now. We can't change any of it." She spoke without looking up at him.

It may have been in the past, but he needed to know. "Would you have told me after the baby was born?" He didn't want to believe she would have kept that from him if she'd had the baby. Still, who knew?

Silence stretched out between them. When he could no longer take it, Nate took a step back, forcing Lauren to loosen her embrace. "Lauren?" Her tear-filled eyes met his, and the pain he saw in them nearly brought him to his knees.

"I don't know," she whispered. "But it doesn't matter anyway. I didn't have the baby, and we both have our own lives now."

He'd come in pissed and hurt. Hell, he still was. Right now, though, that didn't matter. He had Lauren in his arms, and they were talking rather than arguing. "We might have separate lives now, but that doesn't change the fact that I still love you." He'd never been one to be subtle, so he saw no reason to start now. Without any hesitation, he bent his head toward her for a kiss. Lauren's tongue darted out to moisten her lips, but otherwise she didn't move. When his lips settled on hers, she flinched slightly but didn't pull away.

Taking it slow, he moved his mouth against her lips and pulled her closer so their bodies touched from chest to thigh. In response, Lauren slid her arms up and over his shoulders. Then her fingers began to dance across the back of his neck. The gentle caress shot his already aroused body into the stratosphere. With his tongue he teased her lips open. When her lips parted, his tongue slid inside and rubbed against hers. He was no longer in control, and hungry for Lauren's touch. Their kiss became wild. Moving his hands up her back, he dug his fingers into her hair, pulling it from the elastic in the process. The soft strands covered his hands, and memories of lying together with her hair tickling his chest rushed through his mind. How many times had her hair covered him as they relaxed? At the time, he never would have thought he'd miss it. But now with her so close, he realized just how much he'd missed even the little insignificant things with her.

"God, Lauren." He pulled away when the need for air became too great. "I've missed you so much." He rested his check against her hair and inhaled her shampoo.

Lauren's hand froze in place on his neck then she jumped away from him. "Nate . . . I that . . ." she said, breathless. Her face turned red as she stumbled over her words. "We shouldn't . . . I'm with Kevin." She took another step backward.

He fought the urge to swear aloud. He'd thought they were getting somewhere. She sure as hell kissed him as if she wanted him. "If you loved him, you wouldn't have just kissed me the way you did."

"I'm happy with him." She looked over at the dog rather than him when she answered him.

He heard the truth beneath her words. She didn't love the other guy and she knew it. She just didn't want to admit it to him or herself. "Be honest, Lauren. You don't love him." Nate took a step closer. "Maybe you can lie to him, but not to me. I know you too well. There's still something between us."

Lauren swallowed and held his gaze. "I always know where I stand with Kevin, and I know he won't up and leave."

Kevin sounded more like a dog than a boyfriend. "I'm not going anywhere, sweetheart." The endearment rolled off his tongue. He'd never used it with any other woman.

Lauren opened her mouth but said nothing. Instead, she crossed her arms protectively around herself and searched his face.

"Come on, Lauren. Give us a chance." Nate never begged but if he thought it would help, he'd do it now.

"I don't know," Lauren answered, looking away. "I need time to think."

While still not the answer he wanted, he grabbed onto the uncertainty in her voice. If she truly felt nothing, her answer would have been an outright no.

"Fair enough." He forced the words from his mouth. He didn't want to waste any more time. They'd already lost fifteen years. But he had little choice. Before she could stop him, he moved closer and dropped a light kiss on her lips. "I'll see you soon."

***

Lauren stared at the television, her mind a million miles away from her living room. By now she should be in bed. Midnight had come and gone, and before she knew it, her alarm would go off. But even with knowing this, she couldn't sleep. Both her body and mind fluttered with emotions of every kind. The usual anger and sadness that overcame her whenever she thought of the baby she'd lost weighed down on her, but this time so did guilt. At the time, she'd been angry at Nate, but he'd had a right to know she was pregnant. She justified not telling him because he never contacted her, but she'd been wrong. And what if she hadn't lost the baby? Would she have told him then? Honestly, she did not know.

And what about now? What did she really want? When they kissed, it took her breath away. Made her feel alive in a way no other man's kiss ever did. Wrapped in his arms, her mind and body forgot about the past. All it recognized was the man and how he made her feel. But she couldn't let herself forget the past. When he left, it had nearly killed her. Depression had plagued her for months. She'd almost failed her freshman year of college, in fact. Did she want to open herself up to him again like that? What about Kevin? More guilt pressed down on her as she thought of him. He didn't set her body on fire like Nate, but they enjoyed each other's company. He treated her well, and they shared some of the same interests. Kevin was safe, and he didn't make decisions for her.

"What am I going to do, JoJo?" Lauren asked the dog next to her.

JoJo cracked open her eyes at the sound of her name. Then, after a heavy sigh, the dog readjusted her head and closed her eyes again.

"Thanks for all your help." Reaching out, she rubbed behind the dog's ears. She needed someone other than her dog to talk to. In the past, she would have picked up the phone and called Callie regardless of the time. That was the type of friendship they'd had. But not anymore. Sure, she still considered Callie her closest friend, but now she had Dylan in her life. Any phone calls would have to wait until tomorrow. Her sister Kelly was out, too. With the new baby, she needed to rest whenever she could. With no other options Lauren leaned her head back against the couch and closed her eyes. Maybe if she pretended to sleep, her body would get the message and she'd still get about five hours of sleep. Five hours was better than none.

Chapter 7

The ring of her cell phone pulled Lauren from the lesson plans in front of her. She wanted them done before calling it a day and heading home to pack for the weekend with Kevin in New York—something she should be excited about. Unfortunately, since her last run-in with Nate, she wished she'd never invited Kevin along. With her emotions stuck on this darn roller coaster, she needed a weekend away from both men. Maybe with hundreds of miles separating her from both of them, she could get her head on straight. But she'd already asked Kevin, and he had rearranged his schedule so he could join her. After that, there was no way she could cancel on him.

When she picked up the phone, Kevin's name

glared back at her. Right away, hope sprang to life. He never called this early. Was it possible something had come up, and he needed to change their plans? It had happened several times in the past. On those occasions it had annoyed her. If it happened today, she'd do a little jig right there in the middle of her classroom.

"Hi, Kevin." Lauren tried to infuse some cheer into her voice. "Is everything okay?"

A hacking cough came through the phone. "No," he said in a raspy voice. Another coughing fit came over him. "I'm sick. The flu."

Lauren almost didn't recognize the voice. He sounded as if he'd placed a clothespin over his nose.

"There is no way I can make it this weekend. I went to the doctor this morning and have been in bed ever since. If Olivia hasn't gone back to California yet she'd love to go with you."

A crazy mixture of relief and guilt washed over her. The poor guy sounded miserable, and she knew how awful the flu made you feel. She'd had her own run-in with it around Thanksgiving. Yet, thanks to his condition she was getting out of their weekend together.

"I understand. Is there anything I can do for you? Bring you anything?"

"Kill me, maybe," he moaned, before another cough assaulted her ears. "Every part of my body aches."

"I know the flu is brutal. Make sure you rest. I spent three days in bed sleeping when I had it."

"Trust me, unless the house is on fire, I don't plan

on leaving my bed," Kevin said. "If I feel better, I'll call you on Sunday. I'll text you Olivia's number if you want to try her. Have fun in New York."

"Thanks. Feel better."

Lauren stared around her empty classroom. Now that Kevin couldn't go, she had an extra ticket. Should she ask a friend or give Olivia a call? Her first choice of companions was out. Callie hated the ballet. The only way she'd get her there was by physical force. Kelly was out, too. Not many of her friends enjoyed the ballet, but Kevin's sister did. Would she enjoy a whole weekend with Olivia? They'd only met that one time. She'd have to think about it, and, worst-case scenario, she would go alone. Just because she had an extra ticket didn't mean she had to use it.

***

Under three layers of blankets, Kevin shivered again and cursed his bad luck. He could not recall when he'd last been sick. And never like this. Every inch of his body ached, one minute he was hot and the next freezing, and the cough medicine did not even take the edge off. He just wanted to die and end his suffering.

His physical ailments only added to his foul mood. Of all the weekends, it had to happen on this one. While not a huge fan of the ballet—in truth he found it downright boring—he had been looking forward to a getaway with Lauren.

He had postponed his Friday afternoon

appointment until the following week just so they could leave when she got out of school. Rarely did he change business meetings for anything or anyone, much less something as trivial as the ballet, but he knew how important this was to Lauren. Not to mention he figured it was a great opportunity to further develop their relationship. Even before she'd asked him, he had been considering a romantic weekend getaway. Especially considering her distant behavior as of late. Although she never called on a regular basis, her phone calls had become even less frequent. When they did talk on the phone, she sounded preoccupied and kept their conversations short. The last time they'd gotten together, she remained stiff and rigid most of the night. Only twice had he glimpsed the woman he'd first met: once when she discussed the ballet with his sister and then when she slipped her hand into his under the table. Of course, he could chalk up her behavior that night to meeting his parents for the first time.

When she'd dropped this weekend in his lap, it had alleviated some of his worry over the change he'd noticed in her. How important could the guy from her past be if she invited him away for the weekend? Not that it mattered now. Thanks to the damn flu, he was stuck in bed, his hopes of pushing their relationship closer to an engagement put on hold.

Although, maybe it didn't need any further encouragement. If Lauren wasn't fully invested in them, would she have asked him? She could have just as easily invited along a friend like Callie. She hadn't, though. She'd asked him, and she'd sounded genuinely disappointed when he'd just talked to her.

Despite the drummer in his head using his brain to compose a rock song, Kevin smiled. He had nothing to worry about.

***

"That was amazing." Suzanne Miller followed Lauren into their suite at The Sherbrooke Plaza Hotel located in the heart of New York City. New to Ridgefield, Suzanne taught tap and ballet with Lauren, and they had become friends over the past winter.

Amazing was only one of the many adjectives Lauren would use to describe the show. It had been everything she'd imagined a New York City performance to be and then some.

"I could have sat there all night and watched them perform," Lauren said, fingering her gold hoop earring. Her eyes once again took in the elegant suite, an odd sense of unease forming inside her.

When they had checked in the previous afternoon, the hotel concierge had immediately descended on them. Despite her protests that it wasn't necessary, he'd escorted them up to their suite. When she realized their floor could only be accessed with a VIP room card, she'd known Callie hadn't booked her in any ordinary room. Still, when the elevator doors opened she'd been surprised. Nothing around her resembled the hotels she was used to. Then the concierge unlocked her suite door, and she'd stared at it once again, reminded of just how different Callie's life had become.

"I still can't believe this whole trip was a birthday present." Suzanne stood near the window looking down at the city. "Half my friends forgot to even wish me a happy birthday this year."

No question about it, she was lucky to have a friend like Callie. Few people had friends they could depend on the way Lauren and Callie depended on each other. "We've been friends for a long time. She's more like a sister than a friend."

"You're still lucky." She nodded toward the city outside. "What do you say we go to some clubs? It's still early and we're both single. Let's have some fun. See who we can meet."

A few hours at a dance club sounded fun. "I'm not single, Suzanne, and neither are you. Or are you and Bryan done?"

Suzanne rolled her eyes. "I don't see rings on either of our fingers, Lauren." She held up her hand and wiggled her ring finger. "Bryan's okay with me seeing other men. He went out with a woman from work last night since I was here with you."

Ring or no ring on her hand, the last thing she needed was another man in her life. Even now guilt slammed her over the head every time she saw Kevin or talked to him. It might not have been intentional, but she'd now kissed Nate on two separate occasions. Something she had no business doing while still with Kevin.

"You pick up anyone you want, but I'm only

dancing tonight."

"Suit yourself," she said with a shrug. "I'm going to change. See you in a few minutes."

Lauren shook her head and headed to her own bedroom off the living room area. *To each her own.* If Suzanne spent the night with some stranger, she wouldn't get a lecture from her, as long as she didn't bring him back here.

Alone in her room, she hung up the gown from Callie. For a second, she considered calling Kevin to check on him. He had sounded terrible when he called and a good girlfriend would call and see how he felt. Even knowing this, she held back. First and foremost, he needed his rest. That reason alone didn't hold her back, however, and she knew it. So far the trip into New York and the ballet had been a terrific distraction from her relationship woes, but calling him would only reinforce the fact that she had a decision to make.

Should she stick with the safe path and stay with Kevin or risk her heart again and give Nate another chance? Every time she thought she had made up her mind, a memory or a thought occurred, and she again found herself pondering her choices. The way she saw it, both choices had repercussions. If she stayed with Kevin, not only might she find herself in a relationship with a man she never loved, but she'd also have to see Nate go on with his life without her. On the other hand, if she jumped headfirst into something with Nate, not only was she setting herself up for possible emotional devastation, she might be throwing away something special with Kevin.

"What a complete mess," Lauren said as she pulled on her black boots.

***

"You might want to check on those steaks," Nate said, referring to the Porterhouse steaks his brother had put on the grill. Older by three years, Ryan and his wife lived on the opposite side of town from their parents.

"I know how to grill, and they're fine. But if you don't like the way I do it, be my guest," Ryan answered, a hint of sarcasm in his voice.

Nate refused to take the bait, knowing if he got up and checked now, he'd have grill duty for the rest of the night.

"How's it going living back at Mom and Dad's?" Ryan asked when Nate stayed seated. "Is Mom constantly stopping by?"

When he'd moved into the apartment he'd expected that from his mom. Except for the few times she'd brought by his mail because it had been left in his parents' mailbox instead of his, she never stopped over. She called once or twice a week to invite him for dinner, but otherwise she gave him his own space.

"I hardly see them. But it's still just a temporary arrangement. I haven't had enough time to find something else." One more problem on his list.

"Heard you and McDonald got into it at O'Donnell's."

He didn't need another reminder of Lauren. He

had enough of them back in his apartment. Every time he walked into his bedroom, memories of what they'd done in there while in high school ambushed him. In fact, he'd been searching for a distraction from those memories when Ryan called and invited him over.

"Who'd you hear that from?" Who else had been in the pub that night? At the moment he was drawing a blank. The shock and grief had overwhelmed him. If he'd handled things differently that summer, what would've happened? What if she'd had the baby? Would they be a family today?

The shock had since worn off, but not the grief. His heart still ached for what they'd both lost. The only thing that helped ease it was the knowledge that Lauren still cared. Their kiss that night had sent his body and mind spiraling out of control. That kiss and Lauren's request for time to think kept his hopes high. If no chance existed for them, she would have told him upfront. She wouldn't string him along and play games with him.

"We had words. It was no big deal."

Ryan reclined in his chair and crossed his arms. "That's not how I heard it. Harry Evans said he expected some blows. Said he heard McDonald warn you to stay away from Lauren."

Harry Evans had always acted like an eighty-year-old busybody. It looked like some things never changed. "Evans is an ass." He wasn't sharing what he learned that night with anyone.

Ryan shrugged one shoulder. "Never said he wasn't, but he usually knows what he's talking about when it comes to rumors."

Had others heard Matt's outburst? They'd raised their voices but not until later in the conversation, after Matt dropped the news on him.

"Yeah, Matt told me to leave her alone. He made sure he reminded me she was with someone."

"Yeah, I heard she'd been dating some wealthy business executive from Rhode Island. So what's your plan?"

"She asked for time, so I am giving her that." He left out the particulars of why and when she'd made the request.

Ryan stood and clapped him on the back on his way to the grill. "Anything I can do to help. Say the word."

His brother could not do anything, no one could. Still, he appreciated the offer. It helped to know his family wanted them together, but he wasn't going to tell his brother that, either.

"Yeah, you can get those steaks off the grill before we need a sledgehammer to cut them." Now seemed like a good time for a change of topic. Especially before his sister-in-law came home and started poking around.

Chapter 8

"You're quiet tonight." Kevin took the seat next to her, a glass of white wine in each hand. She'd driven to his estate in East Greenwich and they'd driven into Providence for dinner and a play. Now they were back at his house for the night. Or at least that had been the original plan.

Unease about spending the night nagged Lauren. In the months they'd been dating they'd never spent the night at each other's home. Doing so now gave the impression she wanted to take their relationship to the next level, to something more serious. Before Nate walked back into town, she'd wanted that with Kevin. Or at least she'd thought she had. Now, she had her doubts.

Lauren accepted a glass, a forced smile on her face. "Just tired. I've had a lot on my mind that's kept me up at night." She spoke only the truth. She just left out some key information.

Kevin's hand settled on her shoulder, his skin smooth and warm. "One of those weeks? Well, tonight you can relax." He pulled her closer and kissed her.

She held her breath and waited, hoping for a rush of heat or excitement. Kevin's touch brought nothing. Not a single ounce of emotion sparked with him so close—unlike with someone else. Nate merely entered a room and her body reacted.

Stop comparing the two. Lauren snuggled closer. "I'm glad you invited me for the weekend." His invitation had come out of the blue. Before his phone call, she hadn't expected to see him until sometime the following week.

"I hated not making the trip to New York with you, so I thought we could spend this weekend together. I've missed you."

He moved in for another kiss, taking her by surprise. Lauren responded, hoping that at any minute fireworks would go off or doves would start to sing, but she got nothing. Not even a pigeon chirped.

She went with the flow when he coaxed her lips apart. When he shifted his position so he could wrap both arms around her, she moved and looped her arms around his neck. All the while, though, she remained strangely detached. Her body went through the motions, yet her mind remained elsewhere, passing the time until the kiss ended.

The cool metal of his watch brushed against her back when he slipped a hand under her top. Still, her body remained unaffected. And when Kevin pulled back, her eyes popped open, and she found him staring back at her. His eyes searched her face. Exactly what did he see? Could he tell the kiss had no effect on her? Did he somehow know her thoughts were filled with images of Nate?

"Lauren, I want to ask you something." He held her gaze, his voice confident and business-like. Leaning back he reached into his pants pocket.

In slow motion, Lauren watched him pull out a ring box.

Popping open the box, he held it up to her. "Will you marry me?"

She heard the words. Saw his lips move but her brain couldn't put the two together. For years she'd dreamed of a handsome man proposing with a beautiful ring. Now she had her dream in front of her, yet she couldn't reply. Couldn't comprehend the situation.

Lauren glanced down at the intricately set diamond then back up at Kevin as her utter confusion set off warning bells in her head. Nothing had prepared her for this. He'd never once hinted that he loved her. That he wanted their relationship to be permanent. Heck, she didn't know if *she* wanted their relationship to become permanent.

"I . . . Kevin, I don't know what to say." Somehow she managed to get the words from her brain and out her mouth.

Kevin's lips curved upward. "Usually a woman says yes when a man asks her to marry him." He pulled the ring from the box and held it toward her.

Yeah, but usually they love each other. "We've only been together a few months." She fought down the hysterical laugh threatening to escape.

"So? My parents only knew each other a month before they got engaged. They've been married for thirty-eight years."

He trailed his hand down the side of her face. Again, she couldn't help but notice how smooth and soft his hands were. The complete opposite of Nate's. His hands had been callused and dry. The single thought of Nate's hands brought back memories of their kisses. *Not now.* She couldn't let him into her thoughts now. Not with Kevin's gigantic ring in front of her. Lauren jumped to her feet, turned, and took several steps away from him. "Kevin, we don't love each other. At least not yet."

His immediate laugh surprised her, and she spun back around.

"What does that have to do with anything? Marriages are a lot like business deals in my family."

Okay, had she walked into an alternate universe or something? "Business deals?" Maybe she'd misheard him.

In one smooth motion, Kevin rose. "My parents were married to solidify the Walsh and Miles merger. Olivia's marriage to Greg expanded the company on the West Coast. In both relationships they respect each other and support each other, but they didn't marry for love." Kevin moved closer. "We respect each other. Have fun together. Share a lot of the same interests. Get along well. What's the problem?"

He wrapped his arms around her waist. The weight of his arms pressed down on her. "So if marriage is all about business, how does marrying me make sense?"

"I can give you financial security for life. You could stop teaching and open the dance school you told me about. In fact, you could open several. You could travel. See those places in Europe you have up on your walls. You'd be part . . ."

He rubbed her lower back as he spoke, but rather than help relax her, the movement increased her unease. The more Kevin spoke, the more she wondered if she'd left planet Earth.

Lauren pressed her index finger against his lips. "Stop, please. I get the benefits to me, Kevin. But what do you get out of this business deal?" *I'm not going to like the answer.*

Before he said another word, he pulled her hand back and kissed her knuckles. "A solid friendship with the Talbots and Sherbrookes. A personal connection would help in the bidding war for the contract to construct Sherbrooke Enterprises' newest resorts in California. Not to mention the extra boost it'd give me when I run for a seat in Congress in another year."

Her mind flooded with a jumble of thoughts. For a moment, she felt as if she were back in Mr. Tasca's senior calculus class. The one and only class she'd ever failed in high school because nothing the man had ever said made any sense to her.

Rubbing at the sudden throb in her forehead, she took a step back. For the first time that night, she really looked at Kevin. No one would deny that he was a handsome man in a sleek metro way. He always wore the best clothes. His hair always appeared just right. And they did have fun together. They had similar senses of humor, enjoyed the theater and the latest music. He treated her with respect. With the exception of his proposal, she always knew what to expect from him. He was safe and predictable. And at the moment he was offering her the world.

That's what I want. The thought ran through her mind, yet she held back from accepting the diamond. Even with everything he offered, something told her to hold off. A marriage treated like a business merger may protect her heart, but was it what she wanted? Since she'd gotten her first bridal Barbie, she'd dreamed of marrying her own prince charming. A man head over heels in love with her, that she'd have children and eventually grandchildren with. The future Kevin presented didn't come close to her dream. At the same time, though, he could give her everything else she'd always dreamed of. And who knew? Maybe someday they would love each other.

Beneath his hands, her back tensed as the silence stretched out. He'd expected Lauren to be surprised. Never during their time together had they spoken of marriage. Still, he'd assumed she'd accept his offer tonight. Why wouldn't she? Most women would jump at what he offered her. Lauren didn't strike him as any different.

"If you want a long engagement, we can do that. The wedding doesn't need to be next month. We could wait until the fall or after the holidays if you want."

Lauren closed her eyes, her chest rising and lowering as she took in a few deep breaths. When she opened her eyes, she met his gaze but remained tight-lipped, not offering him a single hint at her answer.

"What are you thinking?" Over the months, he'd learned that while Lauren may like to be silly and have fun—her crazy earrings were a perfect example of that—she was a practical woman. Once she thought about what he'd just offered, she would agree to the marriage.

She shook her head, her hair brushing against his hands. "I . . . Kevin, I don't . . ." Her voice trailed off, and she took a sudden step backward, forcing him to let go.

"I enjoy spending time with you. But marriage? I don't know." Her voice wavered.

He smiled to himself. She hadn't said no, and from the sound of it with a little coaxing she'd agree.

"I need some time to think about it."

"I can understand that." Kevin moved back into her personal space but kept his hands by his sides. "Take as long as you want." He could be patient, and in the meantime he'd work on swaying her toward a yes.

Lauren flashed him a tentative smile. "Thank you." Her relief echoed in her voice.

"Why don't you hold on to this for now?" Kevin pressed the ring box into her hand. Before she could offer up a protest, he said, "Let's put on a movie."

Her eyes darted down to the ring and then back to him. "It might be better if I go home."

A twinge of doubt flickered through his mind. "I thought you planned to spend the weekend." He ran a finger down her cheek. "It's late, Lauren . . . stay."

Despite his efforts, ten minutes later, Kevin walked back into the house alone. He bypassed the open bottle of wine and headed toward the back of the house. After changing into shorts and a T-shirt, he hit the weights. He'd learned a long time ago that exercise helped him plan. Some of his best business decisions came to him when he worked out.

By the time he punched out half of his hour-long routine, his annoyance had subsided enough for him to look at things from Lauren's point of view. She would come around at some point, but maybe he did spring it on her too soon. Looking at a marriage as a business deal was the norm for him. In his world, people did it without blinking an eye. In fact, most of the time he didn't consider marriage as anything more than a business deal. Other people did, though. He needed to remember that. He also needed to show Lauren that, even without love, a marriage between them could thrive. His own parents never claimed to love each other, at least not in his presence. Regardless, they worked well together. They complemented each other. His mother left all the business and financial details to her husband, while his father left the social and charitable details to his wife. But Lauren wasn't his mother.

Sherry Miles had come from a family already well-established in society. When she'd met Clinton Walsh, she'd already set her mind on taking her position in society to the next level. From the start, she'd known marriage to Clinton would do that for her.

Lauren didn't think in those terms, which sucked. He'd spent his life around women like his mother. He understood how they thought and what they wanted. His relationship with Lauren threw him into new territory. At times the challenge of figuring her out exhilarated him. Made him realize how routine everything in his life had become, including his relationships with women. Other times, like now, it drove him up the wall. Since he'd met her at a charity dinner, he'd known she could be the catalyst to push him and his company into the elite circle of the Sherbrookes and Talbots. Before that chance run-in with her, he'd never been able to quite breach the inner sanctum where the Talbots and Sherbrookes lived and worked. At the same time, his association with Lauren—and thus her friend Callie Talbot—would help launch his political career.

Kevin took a seat on the rowing machine. Of course, his decision to propose hadn't only been influenced by how their marriage could benefit him. Not only did they have a lot of interests in common, she was hot. In fact, the night they'd met, that was what had drawn him to her. Only later during dinner did he learn she and Callie were best friends.

He exhaled as he started rowing. If Lauren needed flowers and romantic dinners before she said yes, then that was what she would get.

***

Come on. Lauren glanced at the clock again, but only a minute had passed since the last time she checked. Was it possible for time to run slow? It sure as hell felt like it. All she needed was for the clock to hit nine then she would head over to Callie's.

Tapping her fingers against the counter, she watched the second hand move around the clock that hung on the diner wall. The waitress refilled the coffee mug in front of her, and Lauren gave her a smile. So far that morning she'd drunk enough coffee to keep an elephant awake. The night before she'd left Kevin's and started toward home. Half an hour from his house, she'd changed her mind and headed for Greenwich, Connecticut where Callie and Dylan spent most of their weekends now. She'd arrived in a small town not far from Greenwich around five o'clock. Too early to visit Callie, she found the twenty-four-hour diner and had been drinking coffee ever since, waiting for the clock to hit nine. While still on the early side, Lauren figured Callie and her husband would be awake by then.

Lauren reached for her coffee, more to give herself something to do than because she wanted any more. The box with Kevin's engagement ring dug into her leg, a constant reminder of the previous night's events. She'd tried to leave it with him. No matter what she said, though, he refused to take it back, insisting she hold onto it until she made her decision. Fed up with arguing with him, she stuffed it into her jeans pocket and had not looked at it since. Now, as the extra-strong coffee slid down her throat, she pulled it out and slipped it on her finger. Even in the florescent light, the ring sparkled. She'd expected the large diamond to look gaudy on her hand, yet the unique ring looked perfect. As if it'd been made just for her. Knowing Kevin, it had been designed with her in mind. In the time they'd been together she'd learned Kevin liked to have the best of everything. He'd view an engagement ring in much the same way.

She glanced up at the clock again as the cell phone in her purse rang. *Anyone but Kevin, please.* Lauren pulled out the phone. *Should I answer it?* The number didn't appear familiar. Regardless, she answered it anyway. She had time to kill.

"Hey," an oh-so-familiar male voice said.

Before she realized it, Lauren dropped her left hand into her lap so that the large diamond no longer glared up at her. "Nate, hi. What's up?" Since his last visit when she'd told him she needed time, they hadn't spoken. Not that it had mattered. He'd still been on her mind and in her dreams.

"I got two tickets to a Celtics game from someone at work. Interested in going tonight?"

She hadn't attended a Celtics game since college, but before that she and Nate had gone all the time.

"I'm not around today." Under the counter she played with the ring on her finger.

"Right." His single one-word answer spoke volumes.

"I'm visiting Callie." She didn't owe him any explanations. She had the right to go wherever she pleased with whomever. Still, something pulled at her, insisting she confirm that she wasn't with Kevin. "I haven't seen her since the retirement party."

"Tell her I said hello." The suspicion she'd heard moments ago disappeared from his voice.

"I will. Have fun at the game."

He should not have called her. When he left her house, he promised Lauren space and time. He'd meant it, too, but the wait was killing him, as was the thought of her with someone else. Every time an image of her with Kevin popped up, his insides rolled over. So even though he'd intended to give her the space she wanted, when two Celtics tickets fell into his lap, he thought of her first. Over the years they had attended many games in Boston together. He'd hoped some time together at a game again would help remind her of what they'd once shared.

When she said she wasn't around, anger and dread sucker-punched him. Only her admission about visiting Callie helped relieve the coil of dread wrapped around his heart. His Lauren wouldn't lie to him. If she said she was with Callie, then that was where she was. Even if she had been with Kevin, he would have had no grounds for objection. She had every right to spend time with whomever she chose, just like him. In his case though, he had no desire for any other woman. In truth, during their years apart he'd hardly dated, and he had never developed a lasting relationship. On those rare occasions when he did date, it had been more for something to do rather than because he wanted a woman in his life.

What about her? How many relationships had she been in? Had she looked at another man and thought about marriage?

Thanks to his mother, he knew she'd never been engaged. His mom had always hoped they would get back together and made sure she dropped him hints about Lauren's life over the years. He had almost convinced himself she had never gotten engaged because she still loved him. But her reluctance to take him back made him wonder. Maybe the real reason was because she'd never been asked.

Doesn't matter. The important thing was that she had not outright said no to him the other night. She'd merely asked for time and space while she sorted out her emotions. If no chance for them existed, she would have told him to leave and never come back.

He had to hang on to that. Right now it was all he had as the wait slowly killed him. In the meantime, he needed a distraction. That brought him back to the two Celtics tickets on the kitchen table. A game at the Garden would provide him with a few hours of mindless entertainment.

Picking up his cell phone, he dialed his brother's number. Maybe Ryan would be up for a game tonight.

Chapter 9

After a drive through town to kill time, Lauren pulled onto the long driveway leading up to the Talbot estate. She'd remained at the diner as long as possible, but eventually self-preservation won out. If she sat around consuming any more of the black ink the restaurant called coffee, she'd have a permanent hole in her stomach.

She'd visited Callie's new home a few times since its completion, but when she pulled up near the multi-car garage she once again gaped at the structure in awe. Dylan had spared no expense, and it showed. *I could have something similar with Kevin.* While not quite as grand, his parents' estate, as well as his home, was gorgeous.

Marriage is about more than a nice house. Lauren pushed open the car door and slammed it with all her might. She'd never approached a relationship in terms of what she could gain from it. The fact that she just had didn't sit well with her.

Before ringing the doorbell, she slipped a hand into her jeans pocket. Her fingers wrapped around the velvet box. Then she took one more step and rang the bell.

Moments later the door swung open, but rather than the housekeeper who'd answered on her last visit, or Callie, Jake Sherbrooke stood in the foyer.

"Long time no see. Come on in." Jake graced her with his legendary smile and then gave her a hug.

Unable not to, Lauren returned the embrace. Since their first meeting, Jake had been friendly and welcoming. Not at all what she'd expected after years of reading about him in magazines.

"Callie's not up yet, but you can hang out with us till she comes down."

Great. Callie has guests. That's what I get for not calling first. "I can come back later." She liked Callie's family but didn't want to intrude.

Jake gave her hand a little tug. "It's just me and Charlie and Sara and Christopher. Besides, Callie would be pissed if I let you leave."

Lauren refrained from arguing. If Jake and Callie shared any personality trait it was stubbornness. In fact, the Sherbrookes, or at least the ones she'd met, seemed to have a monopoly on the characteristic.

Jake made polite conversation as he led her

toward the dining room. Lauren held up her end, although if someone were to later ask what they talked about she'd draw a blank. Her mind was busy taking in her surroundings. Although not overdone or showy like Cliff House, the Sherbrooke mansion in Newport, there was no mistaking the refined elegance and wealth that ran through the estate. Unlike the penthouse apartment Callie and Dylan lived in while in New York City which favored a modern style, their new home showcased a turn-of-the-century traditional décor. She hadn't thought much about it on her previous visits, but now she wondered what had influenced the design.

Regardless of what inspired the home, the place was nothing like the apartment Callie had once lived in or the homes Lauren normally visited.

"Help yourself if you're hungry." Jake stopped next to his chair in the dining room and inclined his head toward the far wall. "Nancy set out plenty of food."

Must be nice. The sarcastic thought remained safely in her head. She wasn't jealous of her friends, but who wouldn't love to have a gourmet buffet breakfast set out for them? "Thanks, but I'll just grab some tea." The greasy egg sandwich she'd eaten at the diner still sat in her stomach.

"You don't know what you're missing. Maureen gave Nancy her blueberry-lemon muffin recipe." Jake held up a golden brown muffin.

Across the table from her, Charlie rolled her eyes in Lauren's direction.

"I see some things never change." For the first time since leaving Kevin's house, the stress in her stomach lessened.

"If anything, it has gotten worse since Ma started sending him care packages full of baked goods." Charlie winked in her direction. "I'm starting to think he only married me because of Ma's cooking."

"I told you, Charlie. That was only one of the reasons." Jake popped the rest of his muffin in his mouth.

In response, Charlie punched him in the arm. "Be careful, or you'll be sleeping on the floor tonight."

Lauren sipped her tea and struggled to ignore the envy growing inside her. From the outside at least, Jake and Charlie had the perfect marriage. They teased each other, but at the same time showed affection for each other. They appeared to be friends, partners, and lovers all rolled into one. Sara and Christopher did as well. That type of relationship was what she'd always thought she wanted.

What Kevin offered her would be so much different. Could she live with that? If she married him, the world would be at her feet. As his wife, she could obtain so many of her dreams. An image of Nate sneaked its way into her head. As soon as it did, a collage of emotions bombarded her. *Kevin's safe.* A marriage to him might not include love, at least not in the beginning, but that also meant he could never break her heart. *Unlike someone else.* Nate had the ability to not only break her heart but to crush it into a fine dust.

"Lauren," Callie said with surprise from the doorway. "What's up? Is something wrong?"

She studied her friend as Dylan pulled out a chair for her. While it could have been the lighting in the room, Callie appeared pale and tired. "I need to talk to you. I didn't consider that you might have company." In the past whenever they needed each other, there had been no need to call first. Sometimes she forgot how much Callie's marriage changed things. "But it can wait."

"They're family. They don't count. Come on; let's go upstairs." Callie stood again and grabbed a cup of tea from the sideboard. "Well, are you coming?" she asked when Lauren remained in her seat.

"Really, Callie it can—"

"No, it can't. You wouldn't have driven out here if it could wait."

Lauren didn't bother with an argument. Callie knew her too well. Instead, she snagged her tea and followed Callie up the wide central staircase to her and Dylan's suite.

"Okay now, out with it, Lauren." Callie didn't waste any time once they sat down. "What's the matter?"

"Kevin asked me to marry him last night." Speaking the words aloud made the proposal all that more real. Despite the ring in her pocket, she had almost convinced herself she'd dreamed it all up. "And I kissed Nate." She rushed out the second sentence.

Callie's eyes grew large. "Wow! That's great." She leaned closer as if to give Lauren a hug but then stopped. "Wait, what? You kissed Nate? When?"

"Twice actually." Lauren stared down at her hands. She hadn't intended to tell anyone that. Not even Callie.

Callie nibbled her bottom lip. "I'm confused. Kevin proposed, but you've been seeing Nate?"

She had dated a lot while in college and a fair amount since then, but she'd never cheated on a boyfriend. The way Callie said it, though, sounded as if she'd done just that. "I'm not seeing Nate. We kissed once when he spent the night and again the other day. That's it."

"He spent the night?" Callie's voice rose a few more octaves.

Lauren grimaced. She'd forgotten Callie didn't know all the details about the night her car broke down. "The night my car broke down he gave me a ride home. By the time we got to my house the roads were bad. It would have been dangerous for him to leave, so he slept in the spare bedroom."

"Okay," Callie said, dragging out the words. "And you kissed him?"

"It just happened. One second we were arguing and the next kissing." She couldn't put all the blame on him. Yeah, he'd made the first move, but she'd reciprocated.

"What about the second time?"

"I was upset and crying. I'd just told him about the baby." A large lump formed in her throat. "We haven't seen each other since but I—"

"Wait. You told him? Why now? I think you

better start at the beginning and don't leave anything out."

"I didn't intend to. He showed up one night demanding an explanation. Matt actually dropped the news on him at O'Donnell's."

"Man, this story keeps getting worse."

"Will you please let me finish?" Giving Callie a play-by-play account of the past few weeks was difficult enough. She did not need the constant interruptions.

"Not another word. Promise."

"Anyway, I couldn't lie to him, so I told him everything. Then we kissed again. When I told him about Kevin and that I was happy with him, Nate called my bluff. He asked me to give him another chance."

"What did you tell him? You can't stop there, Lauren."

Lauren exhaled slowly and picked at her fingernail. "I told him I need time to think." Rather than help her sort things out, her conversation so far only intensified the uncertainties she'd been battling for weeks.

"Okay. Did you still take Kevin with you to New York last weekend?"

She switched her attention to another fingernail. "He had the flu, so I went without him. He invited me to spend this weekend with me instead, and I planned on doing that until he pulled out this ring." Lauren handed the box to Callie. "Or at least I think I would've stayed if not for that. I'm not sure."

"You said your relationship wasn't serious yet."

Lauren shrugged. "I didn't think it was. He shocked me last night when he gave me that."

Next to her, Callie opened the box. The light reflected off the stone, casting rainbows on the ceiling.

"He's got good taste." She examined the ring for a moment before handing it back. "Do you want to marry him? Are you in love with him?"

She snapped the box closed. "I like him, but love? No, not yet anyway. And I know it's the same for him."

"He asked you to marry him, but he doesn't love you? Lauren, come on, get serious. Why would he do that?"

Lauren had considered that she'd have to tell Callie his reasons for the marriage. "He sees marriage as a business deal. It'd be good for his company if he got married." *Please don't ask for details.* How could Lauren ever tell her friend that Kevin was using marriage as a way to get in tight with her family?

Callie looked like she'd just swallowed a lemon whole. "What about you? How is this business deal good for you?" Callie's tone told Lauren her exact thoughts on the matter.

"Financial security. I can open my own dance studio. I can travel. Whatever I want." Lauren made an attempt at a sound argument. "It's not as if I don't like him. We get along well and have fun. Maybe someday we'll love each other."

Callie sat in silence biting her lip, a sure sign she was processing everything she'd heard. Across from her, Lauren waited and forced herself to remain silent. Part of her wanted to further plead her case, make Callie understand why marriage made sense. How would that look, though? Would it appear as if she was trying to convince herself, too?

"What about Nate?" Callie asked, her tone gentle and patient.

Not the question she expected. Lauren had to reverse gears.

"You said you told him you needed time to think," Callie said, repeating her own words. "If you told him that then you must still feel something for him."

Sometimes Callie knew her too darn well. "I do." Before now she'd kept the truth inside. "When we kissed it was like we hadn't spent more than a day apart. But I don't know if I want to go there again, chickie. If I do and things end again . . . I can't go through that another time. I'm safe in a relationship with Kevin. There is no burning passion between us, but he can't hurt me either. "

"You won't be happy. That type of marriage isn't you. We both know that. Maybe it works for others, but you're too much like me. Before long you'll wish you'd never met Kevin."

Lauren squirmed. She'd known Callie would speak the truth. "Then you think I should say no."

Callie nodded. "At least for now. Maybe keep things the way they are with him and see what happens. What's the rush?" Callie stopped then opened her mouth to say more only to snap it shut again.

"What? Tell me?"

"You're not going to like it." She sounded resigned to the fact.

"Out with it, chickie."

"I think you should give Nate another chance. I know how much it hurt when he left, but you're both different people now. He wouldn't be trying if he didn't still love you."

Tears tickled her eyes, and she forced the happy image of her niece and nephew the previous Christmas into her thoughts. The memory did the trick, and the overwhelming sadness she'd felt moments earlier dissipated enough she could keep from bawling her eyes out. "Do you remember what I was like when he left last time? I can't go through that again."

Callie put a hand on her arm. "You're assuming it won't work before you even try," she said in her most patient teacher's voice. "What if everything goes the way you always wanted?" She leaned closer. "Do you want to risk that for a business arrangement? People don't usually get a second chance like this, Lauren."

You'd be crazy to let it pass. Callie didn't say the words, yet Lauren read between the lines.

"I just don't know." The war between her head and heart continued to rage despite her heart-to-heart with Callie.

"How about you forget about it for a little while? Stay here tonight and relax. Sleep on it. Nothing will change between now and tomorrow morning."

A few years earlier Lauren would have said yes without any hesitation. "You have company." Callie's family never treated her like an outsider, but she still occasionally felt like one.

Callie rolled her eyes. "Please, it's just family. You're practically my sister, too."

Stay there surrounded by friends or return home alone with nothing to do but dwell on her relationship problems? It wasn't even a fair contest. "Okay, you twisted my arm. You've got yourself another house guest for the night, girlfriend."

***

"I say, let the guys stay here and we go out," Sara said. "Maybe dinner and a movie."

Everyone was gathered in the entertainment room enjoying each other's company, while Jake and Christopher played a video game on the television. The sight of the two men so engrossed in the game amused Lauren to no end. Thanks to the media and the way it portrayed the two men, few would ever believe that international playboy Jake Sherbrooke and billionaire genius Christopher Hall spent their time playing video games. But while it might have surprised others, it didn't shock her. Despite their social status, both men were down-to-earth and enjoyed the same activities as other men their age. Lauren knew firsthand that even grown men still enjoyed their video games, at least both her brother and brother-in-law did.

Most likely Nate still does, too. She'd locked all thoughts of Nate away for the night, or she had tried to. Even with her best efforts, the image materialized of Nate playing a game just as Jake and Christopher were. For as long as she could remember, he'd enjoyed playing video games. She remembered him saving his allowance just so he could buy the newest releases when they hit the shelves. And she had to admit she occasionally liked playing as well. Not the type that Jake and Christopher were playing now, but rather car racing ones. As teenagers, she and Nate would sometimes play video games like that for hours.

What about Kevin? She didn't see him in front of screen with a game controller in his hand. She pictured him more in front of a chess board. Not that there was anything wrong with that. She played chess, although not well. She'd never had the patience necessary to learn all the strategies involved. But Kevin was probably fantastic at the game.

"I'm in," Charlie said, breaking into Lauren's thoughts.

"Me, too," Lauren added, locking her thoughts of Nate and Kevin away.

"Is there anything good playing?" Callie asked.

"*Always A Bridesmaid* came out yesterday," Sara answered referring to Mia Troy's newest romantic comedy.

"Oh, that sounds like a winner," Christopher called out.

Lauren laughed when Sara shot him a dirty look. Even after months of getting to know Sara, the transformation she'd made since falling in love with Christopher Hall amazed her. Before that, Sara came across as cold and distant. A real snob with no personality. Now Lauren considered Sara a friend.

"I wouldn't talk. You thought *Gateway 3000* was a good movie."

She cringed at the mention of the new sci-fi movie. She'd seen it herself with a friend. "Tell me she's joking," Lauren pleaded. "That was a horrible movie. The only thing it had going for it was Anderson Brady."

"He made it almost worth watching," Sara said with a wink toward the women in the room.

Christopher began a retort, but Jake cut him off. "Unless you want to find yourself on the floor tonight, better keep your mouth shut."

Christopher focused back on the game and shot the enemy solider on the screen. "Enjoy the movies."

With their plans set for the evening, Lauren along with Callie, Sara, and Charlie headed out for a girls-only evening, which started with dinner at an Italian restaurant. Like just about everything in and around Greenwich, the restaurant catered to society's elite and it showed. The name of the restaurant wasn't lit up in bold neon colors. A canopy led from the sidewalk, where a valet took the car, right up to the carved wooden door. Inside, a maître d' in a three-piece suit greeted them by name and escorted them to a table in a corner of the restaurant. Fine linen tablecloths covered each table in the dimly lit establishment. Fresh flowers in crystal vases graced each table, along with long slender candles in silver candelabras, providing an intimate atmosphere. If all that wasn't enough to make

Lauren aware of how out of place she was, each place setting at the table had enough utensils to fill her silverware draw at home.

However, like the other times Callie had taken her to the places in her new life, Lauren tucked her unease away and followed Callie's lead. So when the maître d' handed her an open menu containing a selection of wines and cocktails, she accepted it with a thank you. Looking down at the menu, she tried to forget about the discreet glances the other restaurant patrons threw in their direction.

Even the restaurants and clubs she frequented overpriced their alcoholic drinks, so when she did order one she favored those that were least expensive. A quick scan of the menu showed she couldn't do that tonight. No dollar amounts were listed next to any of the drinks. Just another reminder of the clientele that frequented the restaurant, and the fact that within this group she was the outsider. The only one who couldn't easily afford her portion of the tab tonight, not that Callie would let her pay. As with previous times they'd gone to restaurants like this, Callie would insist on covering the whole check. Lauren hated having Callie foot the bill for her, and they'd disagreed about it in the past. At the same time, places like this would put a dent in her monthly budget, so they'd reached a compromise more than a year ago. Whenever Callie visited her in Massachusetts, Lauren paid for meals, but when she visited Callie in either New York or Connecticut, Callie covered dinners out. While not the ideal agreement, it worked.

If I married Kevin, Callie wouldn't need to cover my portion at places like this. As soon as she had the thought, she bent her head in disgust. Money should be the last thing influencing her decision.

"And what can I get for you tonight?" the uniformed waiter asked, once Sara finished placing her cocktail order.

"I'll have an Espresso Martini." Unprepared, Lauren automatically named one of her favorite cocktails and reached for her dinner menu. When the waiter returned for their dinner choices, she wanted to be prepared.

"I'll have a sparkling water," Callie said when the waiter turned toward her.

"I'll put this order in while everyone looks over the menu. So, please take your time making your choices. If you have any questions, please ask." The uniformed waiter smiled then stepped away.

"You're not having a drink?" Lauren closed the menu, food no longer on her mind. Callie didn't drink a lot, but in a social setting like this she would normally join in.

Rather than comment, Callie shrugged and looked down at her menu. The dismissal of the question set the gears in Lauren's brain in motion. The last time they'd been around alcohol at the retirement party, Callie had skipped it as well. Not to mention when she stopped by to wish her a happy birthday, she'd opted for herbal tea instead of coffee. Then this morning she'd looked pale as a ghost and tired.

"Callie, are you feeling okay?" Even as she asked

the question, she suspected the answer.

Callie met her stare. "Of course, why?"

"You haven't been yourself."

Before Callie answered, the waiter reappeared. "Please excuse me, but the chef wants you to know that if you cannot find anything to your liking on the menu, he will prepare anything you wish."

We are definitely not at The Davenport. Lauren clenched her fists under the table, hoping to still her nerves. The Davenport, where they'd held her mom's retirement party, had given them a hard time when they'd asked if guests could have a choice of sides to accompany either their beef or seafood dinners. Yet here, the chef offered to prepare something special in the event they didn't find what they desired on the menu.

Across the table, Charlie lowered her own menu and joined the conversation. "She's right. You looked awful this morning and last night you fell asleep early."

Dropping her eyes, Callie chewed on her bottom lip. *I'm right.* Lauren almost sprung to her feet to hug her friend, all thoughts of where they were gone, but she held back until Callie made it official.

"This cannot leave this table, but I'm pregnant." A smile bright enough to light up a coal mine spread across Callie's face. "We're waiting until Warren and Elizabeth come back from South America to tell them."

A strange combination of emotions rippled through Lauren's chest. The joy and excitement made sense. After all, this was her closest friend. She loved Callie like a sister. The pain and sadness took her by surprise, and for a brief second envy surged through her as well. At one time she'd almost had a baby. Nate's baby. The same emotions always came when a friend announced a pregnancy, yet tonight they were stronger perhaps because of her recent run-in with Nate.

Get a grip. Lauren bolted to her feet and hugged Callie as everyone else offered their congratulations.

"I'm only fourteen weeks, but I had an ultrasound last week, and the heartbeat looked strong."

Discussion of a new baby slowed only long enough for the waiter to take everyone's entree order then it went right back.

"I hope you don't mind diapers because I cannot see Dylan changing one. Jake, yes, Dylan, not in a million years," Charlie said, moving the conversation away from how Callie felt.

"She's got a point. I'm not sure he knows what a diaper even looks like. Jake and Christopher could handle diaper duty, but Dylan . . ." Sara shook her head, her voice trailing off. "He's going to need some help."

Lauren agreed. If Dylan managed to change a diaper without assistance the world would probably end. Regardless, even if he didn't, he'd make a wonderful father. What about Kevin? What kind of a father would he make? The thought rushed in, even though she'd promised herself not to think about him again till tomorrow.

If they married, children would follow. In many ways, Kevin was like Dylan. Yet while she saw Dylan struggling with certain aspects of parenthood like dirty diapers and midnight feedings, she pictured him very involved in his son's or daughter's life. His and Callie's children would not only have the best money could offer, but they'd have the love and attention of both parents. Could the same be said about Kevin? If he viewed marriage as a business contract, how did he view parenthood?

Nate would be an excellent father. The thought forced aside her questions about Kevin. He may not be able to provide the same monetary security, but he'd love and protect them like no other.

"What do you think, Lauren? Can Dylan handle diaper duty?" Callie asked, humor in her voice.

Lauren's eyes snapped up to meet Callie's, and the look she got from her friend said it all. Callie knew exactly where her thoughts had gone. "You'll drill it into him, chickie." She forced humor into her voice. "I've seen you teach fifth graders to write multiparagraph essays. If you can handle that, you can teach Dylan anything. He'll be an expert diaper changer in no time."

Chapter 10

Other than her time with Callie and her family in Greenwich, Lauren had kept herself isolated from everyone since Kevin's proposal. She hadn't even visited her new niece. It had to stop. She needed to make a decision so she could get on with her life. However, while marriage to Kevin seemed ideal one moment, the very next it struck her as what could be the biggest mistake of her life. Of course when it did that, thoughts of Nate were involved, which triggered a whole other set of emotions. So, until she sorted everything out, she planned to keep her distance from anyone who might guess something was up. Only Callie knew the situation, and Lauren wanted it kept that way. If too many people got involved, she'd be bombarded with opinions, only making her decision more muddled and difficult.

"What do you think, JoJo?" She stretched out her legs alongside the dog on the couch. "Should we check out the evening news or watch last night's *Do You Have What It Takes?*" The dog rolled over and buried her head between the pillows.

Lauren switched on the TV. "The news it is." Grabbing the nail polish on the end table, she half watched as she applied a new coat to her fingernails and waited for her frozen dinner to heat in the microwave.

"Although details are still coming in, we do know that one FBI agent is dead and another is in critical condition after a routine interview turned deadly this afternoon."

The nail polish slipped from her hand and landed on her jeans at the news anchor's announcement.

"Officials have not released any names pending notification of the families, but we do know that both agents work out of the FBI office in Boston. The shooting took place in a home located in Chelsea this afternoon. There is no word on who they were interviewing at the time. We will provide you with more information once it becomes available." The news anchor looked over at her co-anchor, who launched into the next big story of the night.

Agent dead. Another in critical condition. The words repeated over and over. Her heart jumped from her chest to her throat as she sat frozen, the light pink nail polish dripping all over her jeans. *Nate.* She needed to know he was okay. Ignoring the mess, she raced into the kitchen where her cell phone sat on the counter, and punched in Nate's cell number which she'd saved in her phone after he had called her. The phone rang several times before switching over to his voice mail. She left a short "call me" message then dialed his parents' number. Like her first phone call, it rang numerous times before Mrs. Callahan's voice clicked on and told her to leave a message.

Who else could she call? His brother might know something, but she didn't have his number. Her heart squeezed at the image of Nate in a hospital bed, or worse. *He's fine. He didn't answer because he's busy.* Once he checked his messages he'd call her.

From the other room, she heard the news anchor launch back into the story, telling viewers they'd just learned that the suspect himself had been injured during a high-speed chase while attempting to flee.

"I can't wait." Without bothering to turn off anything, Lauren grabbed her car keys.

Exactly how she got from her house to his place, she'd never know. The drive was a blur of fear and anxiety. Somehow she managed to pull into the empty driveway near his parents' house ten minutes later. From the outside, his parents' house looked empty, and she saw no sign of life in the apartment over the three-car garage either.

Please be home. Please be home. The words repeated over and over as she ran across the driveway and up the stairs. When she banged on the door, a dog inside barked.

When the door opened a few heartbeats later, Lauren paused long enough to realize it was Nate standing there. Then she lunged at him, wrapping her arms around his neck.

"Lauren what—"

As the gut wrenching fear she'd felt mingled with sudden relief and love, she could do nothing but kiss him, cutting off whatever he'd been about to say.

Nate's arms circled around her, and she slanted her mouth over his then tugged on his bottom lip until he opened for her. For the moment, nothing mattered but kissing him. Proving to herself that he was safe. Focused on the man and his mouth, she didn't notice when he moved his hands up to her shoulders until he pulled her back.

"You can greet me like that anytime, sweetheart. But I think I missed something."

Lauren opened her eyes. Nate stood before her wearing a white undershirt and jeans. A heavy five o'clock shadow covered his face, as did a smile. Heat rushed to every inch of her body at the sight of him and the memories of what they'd done as teenagers in this apartment merged.

Explain yourself. She sent the brief command to her mouth. She couldn't blame him for being confused. One day she was telling him she needed time and the next she was attacking him at his front door.

"I saw on the news an FBI agent from Boston was killed." She ran her hands across his shoulders and down his upper arms. "I tried calling, but you didn't answer." She traced his tattoo with her index finger. She needed the physical contact to reassure herself he was unharmed. "Then I tried your parents."

He cupped her cheek with his hand and trailed a thumb over her jaw. "I needed a shower when I got home. I spent the afternoon searching a house that wasn't fit for animals to live in, never mind a person."

Lauren tipped her face toward his hand. His gentle caress both calmed and aroused her at the same time. "When they didn't answer either, I came here. I needed to know you were okay. That I hadn't lost you again."

Nate bent his head toward her, his intent obvious on his face.

"I can't lose you again," Lauren said, sounding breathless.

He wrapped both arms around her, crushing her against his chest. "You won't. Promise."

Lauren got no opportunity to respond before he locked his mouth on hers again. Years of bottled up passion and emotion exploded between them. As his tongue explored and tasted, Nate's hands slipped under her shirt. When he slid his hand under her bra to cup her breast, her legs wobbled and she leaned into his hand.

Her own hands grabbed at his undershirt pulling it out of his jeans so she could feel the skin underneath. When she trailed her fingers up his spine, he groaned then picked her up. Instantly she wrapped her legs around his waist causing his erection to press intimately against her.

Lauren pulled back for air and met Nate's heated gaze.

"God, I've missed you, Lauren." Nate's words came out on a ragged breath.

The same words sat on her lips, as did *I love you*. Rather than say them, however, Lauren leaned in to show him. And although she didn't think it possible, their kiss became more intense. As they kissed and touched, their passion escalated toward the stars. Unwrapping her legs, she slid down him when they entered his bedroom then grabbed the hem of her shirt and pulled it over her head. Nate didn't hesitate and followed suit. His undershirt hit the bedroom floor as he kicked the door closed with his bare foot. Then as one they landed on his bed, tugging off the rest of each other's clothes.

"I love you." The words slipped out of her mouth just as he entered her. She didn't have time to register what that meant as her brain turned off and her body took over.

***

His day had started off shitty and it'd gone downhill fast from there. But this made up for all of it. Nate placed a kiss on the top of Lauren's head as she slept with her cheek resting on his chest. Nothing had prepared him for Lauren's reaction that night. Since their last conversation, he'd made himself stay away, trying to give her the space and time she'd asked for. Doing so nearly killed him. Now it no longer mattered.

As if to reassure himself that he wasn't dreaming, he ran a hand down her arm. Beneath his fingers, her skin felt like warm satin. For the first time in years, contentment washed through him. *I love you.* Her words played over and over in his heart. So many times when he'd been out on the front lines he'd feared he'd never hear her say that to him again. And maybe he'd had no right to hope for that. But damn, now that she was back next to him, he wasn't going to let her go.

Next to him, Lauren's body moved. "I'm sorry, I fell asleep. How long have I been out?"

"Don't worry." He enjoyed holding her in his arms and just looking at her. "You only slept for about ten minutes."

She moved next to him again, this time pulling herself into an upright position. With deliberate movements, she tucked the sheet around her chest, her eyes glued to the far wall. "I didn't intend for that to happen tonight." She kept her face turned away from him, but he still saw the pink hue in her cheeks.

"I know that, sweetheart." He sat up, too.

"But I'm not sorry it did." Lauren looked over at him a small frown on her face. "I love you, Nate. Always have, but . . . " She paused and took a deep breath. "Are you really here for good? If we try this again, I need to know you won't up and leave again in six months."

"I still have obligations to the Marines as a reservist, and they could call me up to active duty again, but this is home now. I'm not going anywhere, sweetheart."

Lauren sat in silence, her eyes moving over his face. What could she see? Did she see the regret? Or the love he felt? Could she see the wisp of fear that lurked inside him whenever he contemplated her rejection?

She looked away again and began a careful inspection of her half-painted fingernails. "Last weekend Kevin asked me to marry him."

Kevin. On too many occasions, he'd pictured them together like this, and each time it left him with an urge to rip Kevin's head from his body. Her words just then caused the same reaction. "What did you say?" Nothing could stop the hard tone from entering his voice. Her left hand remained empty, but that meant nothing.

As if to sooth him, Lauren placed a hand on his forearm. "I told him I needed to think about it."

It annoyed him that she hadn't said no outright, not that it mattered any longer. She was in his bed right now, not Kevin's. "Why don't you call him now and give him your answer?"

"Kevin's a nice guy, and I should tell him in person. He deserves that much. I'll handle it soon. Promise."

She leaned over and kissed him before he could argue. Kevin no longer existed as far as he was concerned. Only Lauren and the pleasure they found in each other's arms mattered as she leaned into him.

Nails scratched at the bedroom door. "Either your dog wants in the room or she needs to go out." Lauren's hand wandered across his chest and he reached for it, holding it captive with his.

"She needs to go out. Maggie's happy on the couch. She wouldn't want to come in here." He wished she only wanted in the bedroom. Then he could ignore the scratching. "Don't move." Planting a quick kiss on her lips, he swung his feet onto the floor. Without searching for his briefs, he tugged on his jeans. "You need anything while I'm up?" If he had to disturb their time together in his bed, he might as well make it count.

"All set." She shifted in bed causing her hair to fall forward covering her breasts.

With his hand poised on the doorknob, he considered going back to the bed and moving the hair away. Another scratch at the door killed that idea.

Maggie was a well-trained dog, despite the fact she'd been abandoned, and took care of whatever needs she had quickly. After a short pit stop in the kitchen for a glass of water, Nate returned to his room expecting Lauren to be right where he left her.

"I told you not to move." He attempted to tease, but in reality disappointment punched him in the gut. Lauren sat on the edge of the bed in the process of clipping her bra. She'd already pulled on her jeans.

She walked around him toward her shirt on the floor. "It's almost nine o'clock. I have to work tomorrow, Nate." Her head disappeared for a minute inside her top then popped out. "As it is, I haven't looked over my lesson plans for tomorrow."

He had an early morning himself. He needed to be in Weymouth by three in the morning for an arrest. Even with that obscene hour hanging over his head, he didn't want her to go. After fifteen years, he could once again touch her, kiss her, hold her. He wasn't ready to give that up today. "Can't you do it in the morning? Leave here early, stop home and do whatever you need to." They wouldn't have any time together in the morning, but at least she'd be next to him when he woke up.

"I'd feel rushed. Besides, JoJo is at home. She'll need to go out soon."

He had no good argument for that reasoning. "Tomorrow night then. Come by after work with your dog and spend the night." He pulled her close again.

"Maybe."

Prepared with a protest, he started to speak, but Lauren placed a finger over his lips and silenced him.

"I need to end things with Kevin. Let him know I made my decision and give him back his ring. I'll call him tomorrow and see if we can meet up. If he can't do it tomorrow night, I'll come here. Sound fair?"

"Tell him over the phone. You can get the ring back to him later." What difference did it make if she told him over the phone or in person? The end result was the same.

She rolled her eyes at him. "Would you want news like that over the phone? Never mind, don't answer that. If I don't see you tomorrow, then I promise I'll see you on Friday."

She placed a feather-light kiss on his lips and his mind momentarily stopped its search for a sound argument. "I don't plan on letting you out of my sight this weekend." *Or my bed.*

***

Did she have an answer for him? Already a week had slipped by since his proposal. Perhaps he'd been overly optimistic, but he'd expected an answer by now. In all honesty, he'd thought she would agree the day he'd asked. During their phone call days earlier, she'd only said they needed to talk face-to-face. She'd given him no hints during the brief phone conversation Thursday afternoon. Well, nothing other than to sound annoyed that he couldn't meet with her until Saturday afternoon. He'd tried to explain that several key projects required his attention. Whether or not she understood was anyone's guess. In the end she'd sounded resigned to the fact. Briefly, he'd considered rearranging his Friday schedule so they could meet sooner. But if they married, she needed to learn business came first, followed by family and friends.

From the driveway, Kevin saw Lauren walk by the large bay window and glance outside. When she spotted him, she waved. He waved back to acknowledge he'd seen her and grabbed the dozen long-stemmed red roses off the passenger seat. He'd picked them up at the last minute as a peace offering. If she was upset because he hadn't made it sooner, they may help. After all, what woman didn't like receiving flowers?

Even from the walkway, he could hear her dog. Lauren insisted the dog was friendly and not an excessive barker. Yet the dog didn't seem to like him. When he came over, it hovered around them. On more than one occasion it had growled at him and barked nonstop until she put it outside. Lauren had even commented how uncharacteristic the dog acted when he came over. Although he didn't think dogs or animals in general were all that intelligent, maybe this one could sense he wasn't a dog person.

"Knock it off, JoJo. It's Kevin." Lauren's words traveled down the walkway toward him when she opened the door. Next to her, the dog quieted but remained vigilant by her leg.

I'll never get why people have pets. He held out the flowers and pasted a warm smile on his face. "With her around, you always know when someone is here."

She hesitated before taking the flowers from him with a timid smile. "She's better than a doorbell, that's for sure. Come on in." Her tone of voice and body language told him little.

"I'm sorry I couldn't get here sooner." No matter what, you couldn't go wrong with an apology. "I wanted to, but the logistics just made it impossible." He moved into hug her but stopped when Lauren took a step back.

"It's okay. I understand." Her words came out slow and measured, almost as if she'd spent time rehearsing them. "But we need to talk."

A warning bell went off in his head. Either she intended to say no or she was leaning toward that decision. Either way it messed with his plans. "I'm listening." Kevin sat down, careful that he kept his posture relaxed.

Lauren paced in front of him a few times and her dog followed. Given a different set of circumstances he would have laughed at the sight. After the fourth pass though she stopped and faced him. "Kevin, we get along well and have fun together."

Yep, she wasn't going to give him the answer he wanted. At least not without some more persuasion.

"I cannot marry you."

"We don't have to do it now. Let's give it a few more months. Spend some more time together. Maybe take a vacation. Anywhere you want. Paris, London, Rome. After that we can talk about it again." He piled on the compassion and understanding.

She tugged on the bright pink smiley face earring in her right ear. "That won't change anything, Kevin. It's just not going to work between us. We want different things."

As if someone stuck a pin in a balloon, his normally well-contained temper exploded and he saw red. Any well-thought-out arguments evaporated into thin air, and he surged to his feet. "Are you really going to throw away this opportunity for some Marine? Stop and think for a minute about the life you are giving up, Lauren."

She looked away for a moment before meeting his eyes. "This has nothing to do with Nate."

"Bull. You've been different ever since he showed up at your mom's party." He placed his hands on her shoulders. "With me you can have anything you want. You'll no longer be invited to society events just because you're Callie Talbot's best friend. With your leatherneck, you'll always be exactly what you are right now. A middle-class school teacher."

Lauren narrowed her eyes, and he let his hands drop. Damn, he'd gone too far with that last statement. If he hoped to change her mind, he needed to pick his words better.

"I'm sorry. That was uncalled for. Please forgive me. But, Lauren, stop and think about this rationally. With me you'll have everything."

She threw him a look of pity. "Not everything, Kevin. A marriage with no love might work for you but not me." She pulled the ring box he'd left with her out of her sweatshirt pocket and handed it to him.

"Love could develop." He kept his hands by his sides.

Pulling his hand forward, she dropped the box in his palm. "That's not enough. I'm sorry."

What could he say? As much as he wanted the marriage to happen, he couldn't promise love. Even without the promise, though, he held out hope. After a few weeks with her Marine she'd realize what she'd given up by saying no and change her mind.

"If you change your mind, Lauren, you know how to reach me." His hand closed around the ring box. *Just don't wait too long.*

Chapter 11

Nate used his key and let himself inside. Almost a full month had passed since the night he and Lauren first made love, and he'd all but officially moved in with her. While some things still remained at the apartment over his parents' garage, all the essentials were here, including his dog. And every night he slept with Lauren next to him. Just the way he wanted it. He enjoyed the feel of her body pressed up against his. A physical reminder even in the dead of night that he had Lauren back. An added bonus of sleeping with Lauren every night was that his nightmares no longer came as frequently. In the past month they'd only occurred once.

When he entered the kitchen, both Maggie and

JoJo rushed toward him. Over the past month, the two dogs had become inseparable. "Happy to see me, or do you smell this?" He put down the meat lover's pizza he'd grabbed on the way home. Thursdays Lauren taught ballet from four to seven and never had time to cook before class. Since his own culinary skills lacked much beyond scrambled eggs and sandwiches, he'd started grabbing takeout for them on his way home.

After he scratched both dogs behind the ears, Nate hung up his jacket and headed straight for the guest bedroom that doubled as Lauren's office.

With her earbuds in, she remained unaware that he'd come home. From the doorway, he studied her. When he'd run into some of his former classmates, he hadn't recognized them, despite growing up together. Many had either not taken care of themselves or simply not aged well. Lauren, though, hadn't suffered from either of those things. In fact, she looked more beautiful now than she had the summer after high school.

The memory of their final day together that summer surged forward, and he fought to push it away. The past was done. Only the present and future mattered. He had Lauren back. No matter what, nothing would change that. He'd make damn sure of that.

Should I tell her? He'd asked himself the same question earlier in the week when he'd gotten wind of the rumor that the Hostage Rescue Team would be holding tryouts soon at the FBI Academy in Quantico. Since the day he'd decided to apply to the FBI, he'd planned to try for the team if the opportunity ever arose. The team recruited only when it needed to, which meant he could be an agent for years before they held tryouts again.

It's only a rumor. There had been no official word in the office. Besides, if and when it became a definite thing, Justin Billings would let him know. Nate had met Justin, a member of the elite FBI team, the previous year when they'd worked a mission together in Afghanistan. A mission that hadn't gone as planned and left two of Nate's fellow Marines dead and nearly killed Justin. Only Nate's determination and stubbornness had allowed him to keep them both alive, despite Justin's injuries. To this day that mission haunted his dreams.

When Justin returned home, he and Nate stayed in contact. In fact, Justin had been the one to suggest that Nate join the FBI and eventually HRT. At first he'd been unsure, but the more Nate learned about what the FBI did in reality, opposed to on television, and the role it played in protecting U.S. citizens, the more determined he'd become about being an agent.

Even if the rumor proved true, however, there was no guarantee he'd make it past the tryouts. HRT only accepted the best, and most of the agents who tried out didn't make it through the rigorous training process. On the other hand if he made the team, they'd have to move down to Virginia. But if Lauren said she would have been willing to deal with all the moves the military could throw at you all those years ago, then she'd agree to a move now. *That's a lot of ifs and no guarantees. Worry about it if it happens.*

Dismissing all thoughts of work, he came up behind her and wrapped his arms around her shoulders. The instant he made contact, Lauren jumped and then tugged her earbuds out.

"Jeez, you scared me," she scolded him, but gave him a brilliant smile at the same time.

"Maybe you shouldn't wear those in the house." He flicked one of the earpieces with his finger.

"Audiobooks sound better to me when I listen to them like this." She stood and slipped her arms around his neck pressing her body against his. "You shouldn't sneak up on me." She pressed her lips against his before he got a word out.

At first, he let her control the kiss. When she slid her tongue against his, though, he snapped and took over. His mind and body registered everything from the feel of her next to him, to the root beer that lingered on her breath, mixed with the scent of her favorite perfume. *Heaven*. Right here with Lauren was pure heaven. No other word did it justice.

Abruptly, Lauren pulled away. "I need to put this on hold," she said with an audible sigh. "These progress reports are due in the morning."

Nate leaned down. "Are you sure they can't wait till later?" He locked his lips on her earlobe and sucked. When she moaned, he smiled. "They'll still be here in an hour or so."

"No, I need to do it now," she said, her eyes still closed. "Maybe you can eat while I finish."

Eating was the last thing on his mind. "Really?

You'd rather work first." He slipped a hand under the hem of her sweatshirt while he continued to suck on her earlobe.

"Later. I promise." She gave him a tiny shrug. "Go eat. I can smell the pizza from here. Just save me a slice or two."

Nate took a step back. "You got it. You know where to find me when you're done."

Both dogs still sat near the counter when he returned alone. At the smell of the pizza, his stomach growled, and the arousal pounding through his veins subsided. Since he couldn't do anything about the desire he felt, he might as well take care of his body's other demand. He hadn't eaten anything substantial since breakfast.

"Sorry guys, you're not getting any of this," he said to the dogs as he pulled out a bar stool at the counter.

***

Her hands were still behind her back on her bra clasp when Nate walked into the bedroom Friday morning wearing nothing but a towel around his waist. Droplets of water clung to his hair and body, reminding her of the sexy eye candy pictures her friends posted on their profile pages.

Wow. Even after all the times she'd seen him naked in the past month, the sight of him took her breath away.

"Like what you see?" Nate shot her a smile when

he met her gaze, and her heart rate spiked.

We have to work this morning. She forced her feet not to move toward him so she could lick the water droplet slipping down his stomach. "I'm glad you don't let your looks go to your head."

He graced her with another grin then turned toward the bureau. He let the towel drop as he pulled out clean briefs giving her a perfect view of his well-formed butt.

"Try to get home right after school."

At his words, she pulled her eyes away from the excellent view.

"I have a surprise for you this afternoon. I plan to be home by three o'clock."

He pulled the briefs up, and she thought she heard herself sigh. It was going to be one long day.

"What kind of surprise?" she asked, her curiosity piqued.

"You'll see," he answered, a glint of mischief in his eyes.

During breakfast she tried coaxing it out of him numerous times. Each time with no success. On her final attempt he silenced her with a kiss, keeping up his assault until she almost forgot he kept a secret from her. But not quite.

"Come on, Nate, just a little hint."

"Just make sure your calendar is clear all weekend." He tweaked her ponytail as he downed the rest of his coffee. "And I am serious about getting home as soon as possible. Don't hang around and correct papers. They'll still be there on Monday, sweetheart."

From any other man the endearment would sound antiquated, but coming from Nate's lips, it made her feel bathed in sunlight. It warmed her from the inside out.

"I'll be here. Promise."

***

Lauren stood next to the laminating machine in the teachers' workroom later that morning. As usual, the obnoxious smell from the machine made her stomach roll. It amazed her. They'd invented 3-D printers, yet they still hadn't created a machine that could laminate posters without making you nauseous. At least her pile was almost done. Only three more student pictures remained. After that, she had one hour left before school ended for the weekend.

Picking up another picture, she fed it into the machine, her thoughts on Nate's words that morning. Her energetic students kept her mind engaged all morning so she didn't have much opportunity to consider Nate's plans. Now with her students at their music class, her brain focused on little else. What type of surprise did he have for her? Especially one that required him to come home early.

Come home? When had she started to think of her house as his home, too? Granted, he more or less lived there now, but neither had ever officially said they were living together. And she loved having him there. It felt natural, right. As if, despite their fifteen years apart, this was how it was meant to be.

The paper she inserted came out the other end covered in the protective plastic, and she tore it off then entered another picture.

"Just another hour until the weekend," Christine, a first grade teacher, said, entering the room. Like Lauren, Christine had grown up in town and, although they hadn't been friends as children, they got along well now.

"Any big plans this weekend?" Lauren asked.

Christine disappeared into the supply closet and reemerged with purple construction paper. "Nah, Nick and I are driving down to New Jersey. His mom had surgery this week. You?"

When the final student paper came out, she stacked everything up. "Not sure. Nate has a surprise for me."

"I'm surprised you'd even consider getting out of bed on the weekend with him around."

Lauren swatted Christine on the arm with her stack of papers. "You're terrible."

"I'm honest. If Nate Callahan was living in my house, sleeping in my bed . . . well, let's just say you wouldn't see either of us on the weekend." Christine wiggled her eyebrows, a huge smile on her face. Just as quickly as it came though, Christine's smile disappeared. "Don't tell Nick I said that, okay? I'm only joking around. Although, I wouldn't mind if he got some workout tips from your man. Since the wedding, he's put on weight."

Lauren had noticed that herself the last time she'd

seen Nick at the store. Even before his and Christine's wedding he hadn't been a thin man, but recently he appeared much heavier. "My lips are sealed."

"Whatever you do, have fun. I want *all* the details on Monday morning."

Lauren gathered up her students' papers as the bell rang. "See you on Monday."

***

The sign on the highway announcing they'd entered New Hampshire gave her little in the way of information, and so far Nate had offered nothing. That afternoon she'd arrived home a little before him, and when he had walked in all he'd said was to pack a suitcase and that his mom would be by to pick up the dogs. Aside from that, he'd not mentioned where they were headed. Since they'd entered New Hampshire more than an hour ago and continued to head north, they couldn't be going to the beach. Although in all honesty, a beach at this time of year in New Hampshire didn't hold much appeal. Now if it had been a beach in Florida, that she could handle. At the same time, skiing was out. Not only was ski season over, but she didn't ski. Nate knew that. They'd taken lessons together in middle school. Nate, his brother, and her sister had been naturals at it, but she'd spent most of the time on her backside. By the fourth day of lessons she'd given up and spent the rest of the joint family ski trip inside with hot chocolate and a book. Not once since then had she strapped on a pair of skis, and she didn't think she was missing out on much.

"Are you going to tell me where we're going or not?" Outside the window the White Mountains rose before them. Even through the rain and overcast skies, they were breathtaking. Instinctively, she searched for the state's famous Old Man in the mountain, something she'd always done when her family and Nate's had camped in the area. But then she remembered that it had fallen from the side of the mountain a few years earlier. The last time she'd come up to this part of the state it had still been visible. Had it really been that long since her last trip up here?

During her childhood and up until she'd turned seventeen, her family, along with Nate's, had camped up here together almost every summer. Had she been here since then? Lauren thought back, but nothing came to mind. Had it really been more than fifteen years since she'd last come up here?

"You'll know when we get there." He threw her a don't worry, you're going to love this smile, but said nothing else as he continued on the Kancamagus Highway that cut a path through the White Mountain National Forest.

"Time to wake up." Nate shook her, his voice invading her nap.

Lauren pulled her face off the window and rubbed the back of her neck. Outside the window stood a rustic wooden sign welcoming them to Middlebrooke Woods. *Middlebrooke Woods*. She hadn't thought of that place in years. It was the place their two families had normally stayed in New Hampshire. Back then they'd come in either July or August, and most years both families had campers in tow. Nate didn't intend for them to camp did he? She'd slept in a tent before, but it didn't rank high on her list of favorite activities, not to mention it was raining out.

"Isn't it a little wet to camp?" She appreciated his effort to surprise her, but she wasn't spending the weekend in a wet tent.

The car continued down the gravel-covered road. "We're not camping. The owners turned the place into a hotel and spa."

Sure enough, when they turned the bend in the driveway a four-story building came into view. With its white exterior and red-colored roof it reminded her of a smaller version of the famous Mount Washington Resort.

At the curb, a valet waited when Nate pulled up. "Both the hotel and spa got great reviews. I wanted to make you an appointment at the spa, but the place has services I've never heard of. I figured you should do it yourself."

"Maybe we can have a couple's massage. Christine, from school, and her husband go for them all the time."

Nate's expression spoke volumes. "Not happening. Get anything you want, but count me out." He opened the car door without another word.

Despite the rustic location, the hotel they entered had everything you'd expect to find in a hotel located in the heart of a big city. Marble floors led from the revolving doors into the foyer. A gleaming reception desk lined one wall, while in another area several upholstered sofas were arranged in front of a granite fireplace. It was beautiful and not at all what she'd ever expect to find on the grounds of Middlebrooke Woods.

While Nate checked them in, she studied the paintings of the area hanging on the walls. By the looks of it, the owners had built the new hotel on what had been the campsites but had kept the individual log cabins located closer to the lake. Whenever her family had come they'd camped, but she'd always thought the cabins looked cute, and she was glad to see they remained.

"If you need anything, don't hesitate to call the front desk, Mr. Callahan," the receptionist said, handing Nate two room cards.

So far so good. They'd both gotten home early and made it up to New Hampshire at a decent hour. The hotel matched everything he'd seen on the Internet, and Lauren appeared happy with his surprise so far this weekend. Now he just needed to pick the perfect time for the next part of his surprise. Should he do it tonight? Reaching into the front pocket of his suitcase, he felt for the box he'd slipped in there just before they left. Satisfied it remained safe and hidden, he re-zipped the pocket before Lauren came back into the bedroom. If he waited until tomorrow, he could do it over a nice romantic dinner. Make it a special occasion for Lauren. Something that she would always remember. If anyone deserved that, she did.

Nate cracked his knuckles on his left hand. He'd waited this long. He'd survive another night for Lauren's sake.

"If they have openings tomorrow, I want a seaweed wrap." Lauren entered the bedroom, a spa menu in her hand, wearing some black lace teddy he'd never seen on her before. "I've always wanted to try one."

His entire body snapped to attention. The only thing he wanted wrapped around her body right then was him. "Think about it tomorrow." He ripped the menu from her hand and tossed it over his shoulder. "Where have you been hiding this?" He raked his eyes up and down her toned body.

"I picked it up when I went shopping on Monday. Do you like it?" Her voice held the tiniest bit of uncertainty.

She really needed to ask? "I'll show you just how much I like it, sweetheart," he whispered in her ear before picking her up and carrying her to the king-sized bed.

He kissed a trail down her neck toward the strip of lace over her shoulder. Sliding one finger under the lace he tugged it down, his lips following the path his finger took. Once the strap passed her shoulder, he moved lower and pulled the material away from her breast. When he traced the exposed nipple with his tongue, she moaned and dug her fingernails into his back.

Before doing the same thing to her other breast,

he looked up. Lauren's eyes were closed, and her cheeks were flush. The sight of her like that amped up his own desire. "I love you," he whispered, before pulling down the fabric hiding her other breast from him.

Chapter 12

Nate tapped into every ounce of energy he had left and sprinted the last two hundred yards back toward the hotel. After Lauren headed off to her appointment at the spa, he'd hit the wooded trail on the resort grounds. The hotel directory claimed it was almost ten miles. He thought the run would not only use some of the time while he waited for Lauren's return, but also take the edge off his nerves. That morning when he'd woken up with her body snuggled close and a leg thrown over his, he'd almost popped the question. In his heart and mind they'd always belonged together. Now he wanted the rest of the world to know it, too. Even with his eagerness to ask her, he'd managed to hold back. Women loved things to be romantic. Or at least according to the movies they did, so that was what he'd give her. Tonight over a nice candlelit dinner in a restaurant that charged more for one glass of wine than an entire case cost, he'd ask her.

Breathing heavily, he walked to the far corner of the building's exterior. Even after the run, he felt as if he'd finished a whole pot of coffee on an otherwise empty stomach. So far the exercise had done nothing but cover him in mud and make him sweaty.

Why the hell am I worried? She's going to say yes. Why wouldn't she? He tried to ignore the answers his brain immediately made to that question. Still, they kept popping back up. They'd only been back together for a month. After fifteen years apart, a month was nothing. Whose fault was that anyway? No one's but his. What if she preferred to just live together more or less like they were now? Not everyone wanted the whole marriage-and-two-kids thing. Just because she wanted it in high school didn't mean she envisioned it for herself now.

Nate retraced his steps toward the front entrance. *Get your head out of your ass, Callahan. She's going to say yes. End of story.* He crossed the front foyer to the elevators. With each step, he banished his insecurities, locking them behind the barriers in his mind where he stored everything he didn't want to think about. Then he focused on the words he should use tonight. He hated poetry. He didn't know the difference between a sonnet and a haiku, but just this once he wished he knew how to string together the perfect words. Words that would express how he truly felt. He didn't, though, so he'd do what he did best, adapt and conquer.

***

"If this place were closer, I'd visit that spa once a month."

He watched the candlelight dance across her face. She'd arranged her hair in some kind of intricate braid leaving her slender neck and shoulders exposed. He didn't know where she picked up the dress she had on, but it fit her to a T, and he suspected it cost more than he made in a month.

"I cannot believe you came up here and went for a run." She shook her head, an expression of mock outrage on her face. "You should have come with me. There were two men in the waiting room."

Nate raised an eyebrow at her. "Seriously, you can picture me in a spa? Before this weekend that word wasn't even in my vocabulary."

A true smile lit up her face, and his heart doubled in size. Lord, he loved to see her smile.

"No, I can't, but I feel bad. I spent the day enjoying myself and getting pampered while you went for a run." She reached out for his hand. "I want you to enjoy yourself, too."

"Trust me, I enjoyed myself last night and this morning." He squeezed her hand. "And I plan on enjoying myself tonight."

There was no mistaking the eye roll Lauren threw

at him. "You know that's not what I meant."

"I brought you up here so we could spend time together and relax. We're doing that, so I am happy." *It's time.* They'd already ordered and both had full glasses of wine. Their waiter had no reason to disturb them again.

Pulling at his tie, he slid the knot down a fraction of an inch then reached for his wine, his pulse beating double-time in his head. "I wanted to talk to you about something." *Yep, that sounded real romantic.*

"You'll need to wait your turn, because I want to ask you something first."

Taken off guard, he blinked a few times. Before he could reply, she went on.

"You're practically living with me now anyway, so I thought you should just make it official. You know, change the drivers' license, get whatever is left in your parents' apartment."

She wanted him to move in. Good sign.

"What do you think?" she asked

He dropped his free hand into his pocket. His hand wrapped around the ring inside, and his stomach inched a little closer to his throat. "Perfect. My turn." Nate pushed back his chair prepared to get up. And do what? He didn't know. Should he drop to one knee like on TV? "I didn't bring you up here just to relax." He began picking the words as he went. "Even when we weren't together, I loved you. I don't want us to waste any more time apart, Lauren. I know I should have asked you this a long time ago." At the last minute, Nate dropped to one knee in front of her and held up the diamond ring. "Lauren, will you marry me?"

For the first time in his life, he understood the expression "time stood still." His hand wavered as he waited and watched. Lauren's eyes grew wide reminding him of a deer caught in the car's headlights. The expression then disappeared as teardrops rolled down her cheeks. Thankfully, despite her tears, a bright smile graced her face. When she finally nodded, Nate took in a breath, only to have it almost knocked out of him when Lauren launched herself at him.

"I . . . yes." She wrapped her arms around him.

He pulled her closer for a kiss, and only when he heard the applause from the restaurant patrons did he pull back. Even in the restaurant's muted light, he saw the color crawl up Lauren's cheeks. "I hope you like it." He slid the white gold and diamond engagement ring onto her finger. Before he had ventured into a jewelry store, he'd spent several hours reading up on diamonds. He now knew more about the different types of cuts and color qualities of diamonds than a man had any right to. Not that it had made the selection process any easier. He'd still spent a good two hours in the jewelry store the day he bought the ring.

"Nate, it's gorgeous. And it fits. How did you manage that?" Lauren sat back down, but her eyes never left the ring on her hand.

"I brought one of your other rings with me so they could size it. I grabbed it before work one day, and put it back when I came home."

She looked up and frowned at him. "You sneaked through my things, seriously?"

"It was for a good cause. Besides, you can punish me later. Right now, let's eat," he said as their waiter placed their appetizers on the table.

She glanced down at her left hand for perhaps the hundredth time since she'd slipped on the ring. The diamond caught the lights from above and sparkled. The ring was gorgeous. Nate had done a fabulous job picking it out.

Engaged. They were engaged. In high school she had dreamed about it. When he left for the Naval Academy she had buried that dream down deep. Even after they reunited the month before, she hadn't allowed the dream out. Now the dream was about to become a reality.

From her spot on the lounge chair, she watched him swim back toward her. After dinner, they'd come down to the indoor pool. After only two laps, she called it quits and opted to watch Nate from the comfort of a padded lounge chair.

When Nate reached the end of the pool he pulled himself up out of the water and sat on the edge. "Doing okay over there?" he asked.

Seeing him half-naked and dripping wet, Lauren marveled once again at the changes in his body since high school. Yet despite his size and his strength, he was always gentle when they made love. Thoughts of their time in bed that morning set off a fluttering of desire. "Perfect. Just thinking about you, us." The other couple in the pool kept her from sharing any more intimate details. "And a wedding date."

In one movement he stood and joined her on the lounge chair. "What about in June when school gets out?"

"That'll give me less than two months to plan."

Nate used the towel Lauren handed him to dry his face. "So? How long does it take?"

Did he not know how much preparation went into a wedding? "Callie planned hers in about ten months, but it took my sister a year and a half."

"Hell, no. I'm not waiting ten months."

At this point she didn't want a long engagement either. "July, then? Callie and I booked a cruise together. Now that she's pregnant she can't go. That could be our honeymoon." Every year since college they had taken a summer vacation together.

A frown crossed his face so fast Lauren wondered if she'd seen it at all.

"July it is."

Even a July wedding didn't give her much time for planning, but she'd make it work somehow. "On Monday I'll call and set up appointments at some reception locations. I'll try for the weekend so you can come. I hope we can find something." People booked locations sometimes years in advance. At this late date, she might have to take whatever she could find.

"Wherever you want is fine." Nate pulled on the T-shirt he'd worn down. "If you need to go without me, that's okay."

Had she heard him right? "You don't want to

come with me?"

Perhaps he heard the hurt in her voice, because he leaned over and kissed her before answering. "That's not what I said. But I trust your judgment, so if you can't make an appointment that works for both of us, don't stress about it. Just go without me. If you see something you like, book it. I want this day perfect for you. As long as we are both there, anywhere is fine with me."

Most women would kill for a chance to make all the decisions about their wedding, and a part of her was thrilled. Still, this day was about the two of them. Nate should have some input. "Okay, what about the ceremony itself? Do you want it at the church where your parents were married? All your cousins married there. Or do you want a justice of the peace?" If left up to her, she'd have an outdoor wedding. At one time she'd dreamed of a big church wedding, but since Callie's wedding in Newport she'd loved the idea of one outside.

"Up to you, sweetheart."

On that one, she kept silent. An outdoor wedding it was. "You're making this too easy," Lauren said, as she stood up.

"If you need help sampling food choices, count me in. That'll be my contribution." He came to his feet and wrapped his arm around her shoulders.

Lauren leaned into him as they walked from the pool back through the hotel. At that moment there wasn't a single thing she'd change. She'd thought she was happy before Nate came back into her life, but she'd been so wrong. Never had her life felt this right. In her mind she had it all: a wonderful family, a job she loved, great friends, and best of all—the love of the one man who'd had her heart forever. While a marriage to Kevin would have given her money and privilege, she'd never trade what she and Nate had for that.

***

Lauren ended her conversation with the events coordinator, put down her phone, and drew a red line through the last name on her list. Now what? Every single reception facility and country club on her list had a red line through it and some of the places she'd added hadn't been her top choices. In fact, the Kirkland Country Club, which she'd just crossed off, had been more like third or fourth tier choice, and even they didn't have anything open until winter. And that was still better than her favorite location. The Garwood, a fully refurbished hotel built in the 1920's on the North Shore, didn't have anything available until next July. When she'd told Nate about the difficulties she was having finding a place she liked on such short notice, he'd suggested they just skip the formal wedding altogether. He argued that a quick ceremony in Vegas would accomplish the same end with much less hassle. She'd told him exactly what she thought of his idea. In true Nate fashion, he shrugged it off and told her to plan whatever kind of wedding she wanted as long as it happened soon.

That had been last week. Now with every single location crossed off the list, she wondered if maybe his idea held some merit. Maybe they should just contact a justice of the peace and get married in her parents' backyard with close family in attendance. It wouldn't be the wedding she thought she'd have, but did that really matter? They'd save money if they skipped a big reception.

She closed her eyes and tried to picture a wedding at her parents' house. The vision of her father standing at the grill with his "kiss the cook" apron on and the picnic table set with a red-checkered tablecloth popped up. As she and Nate said their vows, her nephew chased her parents' dog through the flowerbed, covering the guests with mud in the process.

Oh God! Lauren dropped her head into her hands. She had to find a place. Otherwise, she'd find herself covered in muddy paw prints or worse. *Come on, there are plenty of places out there.* She pulled open her laptop. Even if guests needed to travel a little, it would be okay.

Lauren scrolled through the Internet looking for something that even remotely appealed to her and fit her budget. She was on her third bridal site when the steady drumbeat to one of Callie's favorite rock songs burst from her phone. *Perfect timing.* She needed a break and a friend right then.

"You couldn't have called at a better time, chickie."

"Bad day?" True concern filled Callie's voice.

Lauren leaned her head on her hand. "More like a

bad week. Everywhere I've called for the wedding is booked." Her eyes flicked over her list. "I even called the Kirkland Country Club."

"You hated it there when your cousin got married. Why would you call them?"

"I'm desperate, girlfriend. If I don't find something soon, I'll be getting married in my parents' backyard with my dad grilling. Instead of a suit he'll probably where that stupid apron of his. Won't that just make a great wedding picture?"

A long chuckle came from the other end of the line.

"Knock it off, Callie. This is not funny. I don't know where else to call."

The laughter subsided. "I'm sorry. I know it's not funny, but I was picturing that Memorial Day cookout last year at your parents. Your mom's entire strawberry shortcake landed on the dog's head."

Lauren moaned as the memory came back. "You had to remind me of that?"

"Why don't you just push the wedding back if you can't find anything? It's not the end of the world if you wait a few months."

"Nate's dead set on it happening soon." Lauren paused for a minute. "And, honestly, I don't want to wait either. It feels as if I've been waiting for this forever."

"Then we'll have it here," Callie said, her voice ringing with authority.

"What?" Lauren rubbed her forehead in confusion. "Have it where?"

"My house in Greenwich. The South lawn would be gorgeous for an afternoon wedding. There is just enough shade, and I don't know how the gardeners do it, but every shrub and flowerbed looks amazing. If it rains, we can move everything inside. I'll have Nancy bring in extra help to prepare and serve the meal."

Holy wow! Lauren bit down on her lip until the urge to weep passed. No matter what, she and Callie had always been there for each other. Still, she was taken aback by her friend's generous offer. Callie and Dylan's new estate in Connecticut was, well, the word "magnificent" didn't really do it justice. A wedding there would be like no other. "Callie . . . I . . . are you—"

"Don't even say it," Callie said before Lauren could finish.

"But what about Dylan? Will he mind?" Over the past few years he'd been nothing but kind and friendly, but this was asking a lot.

"Just give me the date, and I'll arrange everything on this end. You just worry about the other stuff."

For the first time all day, Lauren felt herself smile. "You're the best, you know that, right? I owe you big-time."

"I'll remind you of that after the baby is born and I need a babysitter," Callie said, joking.

"Like I won't want to do that anyway."

Chapter 13

"I expect to see you here," Justin Billings said.

"I'll be there." Nate ended his call with Justin and tossed his phone down. *Damn it.* The rumors were true. The team's tryouts started on July 15th, one week before their wedding. If he didn't go now, who knew when the opportunity would come up again?

How did he break this one to Lauren? She had everything arranged for their wedding. Earlier that week she'd finally found a photographer she liked. When he broke the news that everything needed to be changed she'd flip. She'd already worked so hard on the wedding plans.

The wedding date was only half the problem. She didn't even know he wanted to try out, let alone what it meant if he made it. Not that he hadn't considered that already. More than once since he'd heard the rumor that HRT planned to hold tryouts, he'd almost told her. Each time he'd convinced himself to wait. Why bring up something that may never happen? Man, was that ever coming back to bite him in the ass. Now, not only did he have that subject to drop on her, he needed to tell her to move the wedding date. When he dropped those two bombs on her, he might want a peace offering in hand. Even then, he figured he'd spend the next few nights sleeping in the guest bedroom with only the dogs for company.

"Callahan, I heard HRT's holding tryouts. Does that mean you're leaving us?" Frank Chase asked, stopping by his desk. Despite being only thirty-five, Frank had worked as a special agent for over ten years, thanks to his fluency in six foreign languages. "If so, good luck. I hear the tryout is brutal."

That didn't concern him. Compared to what he was about to face at home with Lauren, his time with HRT would be a piece of cake. "Yeah, I heard the same."

"You and Lauren postponing the wedding until afterward?"

"She doesn't know yet." Nate closed down all the open files on his computer.

Frank dropped both hands on Nate's desk and leaned forward. "You planned for this without telling her? Dumb move, Callahan."

Yeah, he should've told her sooner, but it would all work out in the end regardless. *I hope.* "I'm telling her tonight."

Frank straightened up. "I suggest you give her an expensive gift. Butter her up first, then spring it on her. And if you need a place to sleep tonight, my couch is all yours."

He liked Frank, both as an agent and friend, but his tone just then put him on the defensive. "I don't have to buy a woman like you, Chase." Nate gave him a cocky smile before heading for the elevator.

"If I don't see you tomorrow, I'll know why." Frank's voice carried down the hallway.

Prepared for battle, Nate pulled into the garage armed with a dozen long-stemmed red roses and red velvet cupcakes from Rosie's. The way he saw it, the gifts couldn't hurt.

Even from the garage, the smell of steaks on the grill reached him. The woman really did know how to spoil him. Nothing beat a thick steak cooked on the grill in his book. Nate climbed the stairs and ignored the sudden clenching in his gut. "Time to do this," he said as he reached for the doorknob.

Two high-speed fur-covered freight trains collided into him the minute he opened the door, and he only just managed to keep both the flowers and the cupcakes from landing on the floor.

"Perfect timing. Another five minutes and dinner will be done." Lauren stood in front of the refrigerator, her back to him.

"We need to do something about these two." With his free hand he pushed JoJo's paws off of him and placed the bakery box on the counter.

"They only do that to you," Lauren said, tossing her words over her shoulder as she continued to search for something.

"Lucky me," he muttered, moving up behind her and turning her around to face him. When she opened her mouth to answer, he moved in and silenced her with a kiss. His tongue slowly traced her bottom lip before slipping inside. Without any hesitation she wrapped her arms around him and pressed her body against his, her tongue mating with his as her fingernails dug into his short hair. The cool air from the open refrigerator was a stark contrast to the burning heat raging in his body. Somehow he managed to keep his grip on the flowers and pick her up at the same time. When she wrapped her legs around his waist, he groaned as the pressure behind his zipper increased.

After one final kiss, he pulled his mouth from hers. They needed to talk first before they did anything else. "We'll get back to this after dinner. I promise."

Lauren's eyes fluttered open. "You want to wait? Really?"

He looked away, counted to ten in his head, and nodded.

She unwrapped her legs from his waist and slid down his body. "Who are you?" she asked, eyeing first him and then the flowers. "And since when do you buy me flowers?"

On second thought, maybe he should have skipped the flowers, or had he imagined the suspicion in her voice? "Don't get used to it." Through pure willpower, he forced a smile.

She accepted the bouquet. "I won't," she said and kissed him on the cheek. "Since you want to eat *now*, go on outside, and I'll be right out."

That night they enjoyed dinner on the deck. Earlier in the week Lauren had strung lights around the deck railing and the lights, along with the candles on the table, gave the tiny backyard deck a romantic glow. Despite the setting, beautiful companion, and delicious food, Nate went through the entire meal on autopilot. He cut and chewed his food but didn't taste it. He nodded and agreed as necessary to Lauren's conversation but didn't hear it. His thoughts remained locked on the conversation they still needed to have. The one he didn't know how to start.

"I picked out bridesmaid dresses today." Lauren changed the subject to the wedding for the first time all night. "I went with the lilac. I wanted the yellow, but it didn't look good on everyone."

The shit's about to hit the fan. Nate took a swig of his beer. "We need to change the date of the wedding, Lauren." Sugarcoating the truth would do no good.

Lauren laughed and broke her cupcake in half. "Real funny."

He hadn't expected her not to believe him. "Lauren, I'm not joking." He reached across the table and took her hand. "We need to push it up. I need to be in Quantico on the 15th."

"Can't it wait till after the wedding? What are you going down there for anyway?"

"HRT's tryouts. I got official word today."

Lauren reached for the guitar pick earring in her left ear. "Speak English, Nate. What's HRT?"

"The FBI's Hostage Rescue Team." So far Lauren had remained remarkably calm through the conversation. "It's the Special Forces of the FBI," he added, when the confused look remained on Lauren's face.

"And every office has one of these teams?" The words came out slowly, and he knew he needed to share the rest.

"No. The team is divided into three units, but all are stationed down in Quantico. If I make it, we'll move down there."

Lauren nodded once as she withdrew her hand from his. "There is no if about it. When you decide to do something you never fail, Nate. We both know that."

The sound of her voice, distant and emotionless, sent icy spikes of dread up his spine. "Anything is possible. It's a rigorous trial. Most agents don't make the cut."

"You said you just got official word today. So you've known about this for a while, haven't you?"

The fact that she didn't appear overly concerned about the wedding date worried him. He'd expected an argument about pushing the date up. He had not anticipated her main concern to center on his possible reassignment.

"I've planned on trying for the team since I applied to the FBI, but I didn't know if I'd ever get the chance. Right before we went up to New Hampshire a rumor started going around that they were holding tryouts this summer."

"So, that whole line you gave me about being back for good was bull? You've always known you would leave." Lauren walked away from the table. When she reached the railing she turned back around. "You asked me to marry you and didn't bother to tell me any of this first?"

"When I said that, I meant it. The team doesn't hold tryouts on a regular basis, so I didn't know if I'd ever get the chance. Besides, the team is selective. They don't pick everyone." Shouting and outbursts of anger he could handle. This cold, detached attitude he didn't know how to approach. "When I heard the rumor, I figured it didn't matter. Who cares where we live anyway? You always said you wanted to move away from New England." Nate joined her by the railing, but when he reached for her she avoided his arms.

"I was a teenager when I said that."

"Come on, Lauren. This doesn't really change our plans." He reached for her again. This time he got his arms around her waist. "We'll get married before I go. If I make it we'll buy a house down there and move. If I don't we'll stay here until we need a bigger place."

Lauren laughed, a bitter hollow sound that had him tightening his hold on her.

"You just don't get it. You're still thinking of only yourself just like before. Maybe I don't want to move. My life is here, Nate."

"It's Virginia, not the North Pole. You can make the drive in less than a day."

Before he could stop her, she pushed away from his arms. "I don't know if I can do this."

She slipped the engagement ring off her finger and his heart parachuted out of his chest. "Come on, sweetheart. You don't mean that. You're mad. I get it. Let's talk about it and then get some sleep. Tomorrow I'll help you change everything for the wedding."

She pulled his hand toward her and dropped the ring in his open palm. "Nate, there's nothing to talk about."

Fear and frustration collided head-on inside him. "Don't do this."

Lauren's tear-filled eyes met his. "I didn't do anything. You did. Once again, you figured you knew what was best for both of us. Just like after high school."

"That's—"

"I need some space. You can sleep in the guest room tonight." She wiped the tear away from her cheek. "I'll go to Newport this weekend by myself. When I come back, you can't be here."

His legs suddenly sprouted roots. He watched in silence as she walked into the house and closed the door behind her. Lauren loved him. He clenched his fists, the diamond ring biting into his skin. Tomorrow they'd talk and get everything straightened out. She just needed a little time tonight.

Lauren wrapped the down comforter around her.

Even with the early June temperature and heavy material she shivered. The cold she felt had nothing to do with her environment. It radiated from the gaping hole around her heart.

Rolling over, her cheek hit the other pillow. The scent of Nate's shampoo and soap filled her senses, and she pushed the pillow off the bed. He'd only been living with her a short while, but without him the bed felt empty. *She* felt empty, as if a hand had reached into her chest and yanked her heart out. How had she let him do it to her again? Why had she ever let him back in?

When he left the first time, it had taken months to get on with her life. Why had she risked that again? Sure, this time he wasn't leaving in the same way, but once again he'd gone and made a significant life-altering decision without consulting her first. He knew her life was here. He should have told her upfront about the possibility of a move to Virginia.

If he'd told me . . . Lauren's thoughts trailed off. She would have what? Not let him back into her life? She didn't know anymore. She loved him. Always had. But how could they have a relationship when he made all the decisions? How could they last when he kept secrets from her? Even with as much as they loved each other—and she didn't doubt that he loved her—it wouldn't work if he always put his needs and desires first. Marriage needed to be a partnership between two people who loved each other, not a dictatorship with Nate calling all the shots.

Another round of tears pressed against her eyes.

"Turn it off for tonight." Tomorrow the pain would still be there. Tonight she needed some sleep.

***

Her alarm clock read ten o'clock. By now the coast would be clear. The latest Nate had ever left for work was eight. Besides, she had plans for the day. She'd taken her last personal day off so she could drive down to Newport. The week before, Sara had called inviting her and Nate to Cliff House a day early so the two of them, along with Charlie, could plan a baby shower for Callie. Though sooner than necessary, it made sense to meet now and plan, since they were all attending a fundraiser at Cliff House that Saturday night anyway.

Before she could even consider packing for her weekend trip, she needed coffee and something for her splitting headache. A night of crying had done only two things: given her a monster-sized headache and red eyes.

He won't still be here. Lauren pulled open the bedroom door. Across the hall the guest bedroom door stood open and the bed was neatly made. The entire house remained quiet, like it had always been before Nate moved in. *He's gone.* She exhaled. Thank goodness. She couldn't face him this morning.

Behind her, JoJo's toenails clicked on the hardwood floor, the only sound as she headed toward the kitchen. The scent of coffee still lingered in the air.

The floor beneath her bare feet changed from

wood to tile. The minute her feet hit the cold tile, she froze.

"I just made another pot," Nate said. He sat at the counter, an empty plate before him and a coffee mug in his hand. He'd showered and dressed but appeared in no rush to go.

Lauren unglued her feet then crossed to let the dog outside without meeting his eyes. "Thanks. I need it." Her eyes focused on the picture near the sink as she opened a cabinet. When her skin began to tingle, she knew without turning around that Nate stood behind her. Still, she ignored him and grabbed a mug. When his hand wrapped around her upper arm she paused but still refused to turn around.

"Talk to me, Lauren."

Her shoulders slumped. "There's nothing to talk about. I told you last night. I need some space."

"For how long?" His voice took on a note of desperation.

Days, months. Who knew? "I don't know," she said, her voice soft.

With no warning, he spun her around so that they faced each other. She saw the dark circles under his eyes, evidence that he'd had as bad a night as she. "Damn it. That's not good enough. I love you, you love me. Whatever the problem, let's settle it now so we can move on. I need to be in Virginia next month. I want us married before I go."

Did he not understand the meaning of *I need space*? "Then you should have thought of that before you made decisions for us without asking me. You've done it twice now. This time I'm calling the shots, Nate." She poked him in the chest. "When I figure it out, I'll let you know." Before he could add anything, she yanked her arm away. "I need to get ready." Grabbing her coffee off the counter, she marched back to her room.

Seconds later, the bedroom door swung open and crashed into the wall. *Why didn't I lock it?* Crossing her arms, she waited.

"I don't want things left like this between us."

His tortured expression pulled at her heart. She didn't want to hurt him, but she needed time. His latest news and actions threw her emotions into a new tailspin.

"Can you wait until later to leave so we can talk tonight? I'll come home early as planned." Nate never pleaded. Right now his voice bordered on it.

Some of her anger faded. He really didn't realize he'd been in the wrong. "It's not about talking." She let her arms fall by her sides. "It's about what I need, Nate."

"Lauren . . . " His voice trailed off as he nodded and walked into the room. "This is yours." He dropped the ring on her bureau. "Have a safe trip." He placed a kiss on her cheek. "I love you."

Lauren's heart cracked open, and words failed her as he walked back out of the bedroom. Then she heard the kitchen door open. Alone at last, she sank onto the bed. Dropping her head into her hands, she let the tears come. God, she'd come so close to having her dream come true. Now, thanks to his arrogance, it was in jeopardy. Maybe Kevin and his family had the right idea about marriage after all. Maybe it shouldn't be about love. A marriage formed like a business kept your heart safe.

"Enough crying for now." She raised her head and wiped the tears from her face. She had too much to do before she left, including a call to Callie to tell her the wedding was off.

Chapter 14

Cliff House sprawled out before her. Designed to resemble Alexander Palace in Russia during the late 19th century, the mansion amazed her every time she saw it. The amount of time and money that went into constructing and maintaining the building boggled the mind. Just a few years earlier, she and Callie toured mansions like this one, awestruck by their beauty and the people who had once owned them. Now she got to sleep in places like this on a regular basis, and her best friend and her family owned them. How quickly life changed. Too bad it didn't always change for the better, as it had in Callie's case. She'd gone from thinking her father was dead, to meeting a family she didn't know she had, and meeting the love of her life.

Now she and Dylan were starting a family of their own.

Lauren parked in front of the mammoth garage, a building bigger than her house. *Time to put on a happy face*. Tomorrow when Callie arrived, she could spill her heart, but for now she needed to keep it together.

The Sherbrookes' butler opened the door and, as usual, greeted her in his monotone voice. Someday she'd love to see the guy get angry. He always appeared so calm. Almost to the point of being bored.

"Great. You're here." Sara appeared behind the butler. "Charlie and Allison are here, too."

Sara gave her a welcoming hug. Once again, Lauren thought of how much things had changed. Not that long ago Sara would have said hello and kept on walking. Now, though, she treated Lauren as a friend.

"Allison called me and asked if she could help," Sara explained, referring to Allison Sherbrooke, her and Callie's cousin. "They're outside."

Sara led her out onto the veranda where Charlie and Allison sat, the remnants of lunch still on the table. Immediately, Lauren took a deep breath and enjoyed the smell of the ocean. Off in the distance she saw the sailboat Jake kept moored at the estate, bobbing up and down as the waves crashed against its side.

"Are you hungry? We just finished lunch, but I can have something prepared for you." Sara took a seat next to her cousin. The two women looked so much alike they could be sisters.

"I'm good." Lauren hadn't eaten since the night

before, but even still she had no appetite.

With a nod, Sara pulled the tablet computer from the case by her feet. "Now that Lauren's here we can start." Her fingers flew across the screen, causing the light glittering off the large diamond ring to hit Lauren square in the eye.

"Is that what I think it is?" she asked, all thoughts of Callie's baby shower pushed aside for the moment.

A giddy smile formed, and Sara nodded.

"Why haven't I read about it?" The media loved the Sherbrooke family. How had they missed that Sara Sherbrooke and Christopher Hall were engaged?

"After our trip to Connecticut, we stopped at Martha's Vineyard for a few days, and he asked me then. We haven't told anyone except family yet."

"Congratulations. Can I see?"

The ring on Sara's hand was breathtaking. She couldn't even imagine how many karats the thing was. Actually, in a way it reminded her of the ring Kevin had proposed with, although that one hadn't been quite as large. Despite the beauty of Sara's ring and the one Kevin had offered, she preferred Nate's. She glanced down at her own hand. She hadn't worn the engagement ring long, but her hand looked strange without it now.

"It's beautiful. I won't tell anyone." She released Sara's hand.

"I know. I trust you, Lauren. Congrats, yourself. Callie told me about your wedding next month."

"You and . . ." Charlie paused, her forehead creased as she thought. "Kevin, right? Callie thought you two weren't that serious."

"Who's Kevin? Callie said your fiancé's name was Nate. Someone you grew up with."

Obviously Callie talked about her with her family. But then again, Lauren sometimes did the same. Still, this time she wished her friend had kept her mouth closed.

"Kevin asked me, but I said no. And as of right now, I'm not marrying anyone. I canceled the wedding." Or at least she planned to. She still needed to drop the news on Callie.

Three identical expressions of shock stared back at her.

Sara put down the tablet in her hands, a clear sign that thoughts of the baby shower were gone. "Why? Callie told me the whole story. It sounded as if you were meant for each other."

"When he asked me to marry him, he left out a few details, including that we'd have to move to Virginia if he makes the FBI's HRT."

"What exactly is that?" Allison asked.

"According to Nate, it's the FBI equivalent to the military's special forces," Lauren answered. "Anyway, he made all these decisions before he asked me and now expects me to just go along with them. I can't be with someone who calls all the shots without considering how it will affect me. He did it once before. I'm not letting him do it again."

Sara slipped an arm around her shoulders. "Men are idiots sometimes."

"I heard that." Jake walked out onto the veranda,

followed by his best friend and future brother-in-law Christopher.

"It's the truth," Charlie added when Jake placed a kiss on her cheek.

"If women were in charge, the world would run much smoother," Allison said, adding her two cents to the discussion.

Christopher held up his hands in mock surrender. "Jake, I think that's our cue to leave." He leaned toward Sara and kissed her. "Your brother says his golf game has improved. I'll be back after I prove him wrong."

Lauren watched with envy. Both couples exhibited utter love and happiness. Sure, they probably had disagreements. What couple didn't? But they loved each other. Worked together to keep their relationship on track. At least from where she sat, neither Jake nor Christopher called all the shots, and from what she knew of Sara and Charlie, they'd never let their partners make all the decisions. Was it too much to ask for the same thing with Nate?

"Christopher's in for a big surprise. Jake's game really has improved," Charlie said once the two men departed. "He hired some former PGA golfer to coach him."

"Couldn't take losing to Christopher anymore?" Sara asked.

"Nope. You know your brother."

Sara laughed. "At least they're gone for now." Her smile faded. "Are you sure about canceling the wedding? Maybe you can work things out. And moving might be fun. I worried about moving to California, but now I love it."

"Virginia is beautiful, very similar to Massachusetts, and Quantico isn't that far from us," Charlie added.

Lauren traced a path through the condensation on her water glass. The other women's concern touched her, but weren't they supposed to be planning a baby shower? "It's not only the move. He never once mentioned his plans to me. He assumed I'd just go along with them. That he knew best." She took a sip of water, hoping the lump in her throat would disappear. "When we broke up after high school he did the same thing. He assumed life as a military wife would be too hard on me."

"On that one, I think he was thinking of how hard it would be on him, too. Trust me, I've seen it firsthand. It's just as hard on the husbands and boyfriends when they get deployed as the woman they leave behind," Charlie said.

As a former doctor in the Navy, Lauren trusted Charlie's insight, but that didn't change the past. Before he left for Annapolis all those years ago, they could have discussed it. He could have shared his worries with her.

"From what Callie told me about you two, it sounds like he's the one. Okay, he left after high school. Everyone does stupid things when they're eighteen. He came back to fix his mistake. And if he didn't mention the possibility of a move, he probably just forgot about it. Or assumed you expected a move at some point. Doesn't the FBI move agents all the time?"

Sara's words held at least some truth. Everyone did make mistakes at eighteen. Still, she couldn't dismiss what he'd done when it came to their current situation. "According to Nate, they don't move agents as much as you think. Regardless, when I gave him back the ring, I told him I needed time to think," she said, finally able to get a word in. "He's leaving on July 15th. So no matter what I decide, I need to cancel the wedding."

"Just one more thing, and I promise I won't say anything else. I almost lost Christopher because I let something from my past influence me. Sometimes you need to let go of the past, to forget about it," Sara said.

As promised, after Sara's final comment no one mentioned anything else about Lauren's romantic problems. Instead, the four of them dove into preparations for an end-of-summer baby shower. Even with the conversation centered on perfect locations and color schemes for the shower, part of Lauren remained detached. Even before their conversation, she wondered how she should handle Nate. With him back in her life she felt complete again. Before he'd walked into her mom's retirement party, she hadn't realized just how much she'd missed him. The years had dulled the pain caused by his departure. And looking back, she could admit that over the years she had compared all the men she dated to him. No matter who they were or what they did, none had made her feel the same way Nathaniel Callahan did.

Even with all that, though, could she ignore his insistence on calling all the shots? She wanted a partner, not a guardian. If she married Nate, what kind of future would she have? Would he eventually try to control every aspect of their life? Some men were like that. They didn't allow their wives to make any decisions on their own. She didn't think Nate would ever go that far, but what if this most recent action turned out to be just the beginning? She would never stand for behavior like that, and if they had children she didn't want her children raised in that kind of environment.

***

How had his week gone down the crapper so fast? Monday he'd been on the top of the world. He'd been about to marry the one woman he'd always loved. Then HRT announced tryouts down in Quantico. Since he first applied for a position with the FBI, he'd wanted a spot on the Hostage Rescue Team.

Now just a day later, and he was stuck in traffic with his wedding called off and Lauren expecting him to move out by the time she returned from Newport. Part of him said she'd come to her senses. That she would change her mind and still marry him. What if she didn't, though? Deep down, in a place he avoided, he knew it was possible.

The car in front of him moved, and Nate took his foot off the brake. Why had he scheduled this last minute interview in Natick at four-thirty in the afternoon? Traffic on Route 9 sucked in the middle of the week, but on a Friday the nightmare only intensified. Nate made it to the traffic light just as it turned red.

"Won't miss traffic like this when I move to Maine," Joe said. In his fifties, Joe Perkins had been with the agency for twenty-five years and planned to retire in the fall. Since Nate had arrived in Boston, he'd acted as a mentor of sorts to him. "Heard I'm not the only one moving on. When do you leave?"

"Next month." Nate tapped his fingers against the steering wheel. There had to be a better way around this section of town. Next time he came through here he needed to find it.

"Word of advice. Make sure your fiancée is on board with this. I spent fifteen years with the team, and I saw a lot of marriages end. Even those that looked rock solid from the outside. Heather and I did fine, but not all women can handle the stress."

Nate tucked away Joe's words for later. He hadn't considered how the day-to-day stress of the job would affect Lauren.

"Would've had more kids if I stayed an agent in a field office rather than join the team. But after Nadine was born, Heather said she didn't want to have any more children. In a lot of ways, she was a single parent and she couldn't handle more than Jessie and Nadine."

In the months they'd worked together, Joe rarely divulged any information about his family. In fact before now, Nate hadn't even known the name of Joe's children. For him to do so now spoke volumes.

From where he sat, it sounded as if Joe believed only single agents with no ties belonged with HRT.

"Trying to talk me out of it, Joe?" Nate pulled into the parking lot of an office complex.

"Never. Just preparing you. Life in a field office can't prepare you for life with HRT. So before you take the plunge, make sure you think it through."

***

The entire house was dark when he pulled into the driveway. Not even an outside light remained on, a reminder that Lauren wasn't home. Since he'd moved in, she'd gotten into the habit of leaving the driveway light on for him on those nights he got home late. He'd started to think of it as a welcoming beacon. The absence of that light tonight only drove home how close he was to losing her again.

When Nate walked inside the kitchen Maggie and JoJo immediately greeted him, their tails wagging. The two dogs had become inseparable. Tomorrow when he moved back to his apartment, Maggie wasn't going to like it. And the dog wasn't the only one. No place he'd lived since joining the Marines had felt like home until now, and all because Lauren was there.

Is it worth it? He replayed Joe's words from the afternoon. Yeah, he wanted this, but was it worth risking his and Lauren's future for it? If he spent the rest of his career working cases in Boston, he'd be satisfied. Would it be as thrilling? Would there be the same adrenaline rushes? Hell, no. But he did have other options. An email had gone out yesterday about the SWAT team tryouts. A spot on that would allow him to stay in Boston and still fulfill his desire for a bit more excitement. Not only that, but from the sound of it, it would put far less stress on their relationship. Not that Lauren couldn't handle it, but was it fair for him to do that to her? Especially without preparing her for it? Maybe if he'd told her about it from the start. If he'd done that rather than making his own assumptions, they could have discussed it. If he'd done that she would've had a chance to digest the idea before he uprooted her life.

What he should have done, no longer mattered. The mistake was made. Now he needed to find a way to fix it.

Pulling a beer out of the refrigerator, Nate headed for the living room. With Lauren gone, the house felt like a tomb. He needed some background noise, anything on television would do tonight. He knew the Sox had another game tonight against the Yankees. It was the third game in a four-game series. Only that past Wednesday night they'd cuddled together on the couch watching the Sox beat the Yankees. They'd talked about catching a few games at Fenway that summer. Maybe even asking Callie and Dylan to join them.

Now, that whole night seemed like another lifetime. *Nice job fucking things up.* Tipping back the bottle, he took a swig as the dogs jumped up on the couch next to him. What if he stayed put? Passed on HRT. He reached out and scratched Maggie under her collar. In response, the dog dropped her head on his lap, her eyes closed. "Too bad I can't make Lauren happy this easily." He glanced down at the dog and then turned up the volume on the television as the announcer rattled off the starting lineup for the game.

The voice from the TV became little more than white noise as he sorted out the questions in his head. Would she stay with him if he didn't report to Quantico next month? *Only one way to find out.* She asked for time and space. He'd give her until Sunday night—then he'd make his offer. If she wanted, he'd pass on HRT. A life with her meant a hell of a lot more to him. In the meantime he had no intention of moving out. When she returned from Newport he'd be right here waiting for her, ready to fight for her. Because the truth was, he had no life without her. He'd already tried that, and the thought of going back to it left him numb.

***

She stared into the empty mug, her mind on the conversation from lunch. Both Charlie and Sara had given her a lot to think about. Before Charlie's comment, she'd never considered that Nate broke up with her because he would have found a relationship too difficult while in the Marines. Now though, she saw there may have been multiple reasons for what he did. Sara's warning also resonated with her. If she let her anger from the past influence her decision now, she may regret it later. If she sent him away now, she'd likely never get another chance with him. Was that really what she wanted?

"Hey, I thought I was the only one up." Allison walked into the kitchen and went straight to the refrigerator.

Lauren shot her a weak smile. "Couldn't sleep, so I came down for some warm milk with cinnamon."

"Does that work?"

"Sometimes. Not so much tonight."

"I wanted to tell you this earlier but you seemed done with the conversation." Allison dropped into the seat next to her. "Guys don't think the same way we do. Trust me, I have four brothers. Sometimes I wonder if they think at all."

"Four, ouch. I'm sorry. I have one, and that's more than enough."

The comment elicited an immediate laugh. "You have no idea. Anyway, today you said your boyfriend left out a few details when he proposed. Maybe it was unintentional."

"How—"

Allison held her spoon up as a signal for Lauren to stop. "One sec, I'm getting to that. My brother Trent would've done the same thing. He focuses on the here and now, not the what-ifs. If your boyfriend is anything like Trent, he failed to tell you because it was a what-if. It didn't play into his immediate plan." Allison scooped up a spoonful of chocolate pudding as Lauren digested the words.

Snippets from her conversation with Nate surfaced. He'd admitted that when he proposed tryouts hadn't been announced. Was Allison's theory correct? Had it been less a matter of his making all the decisions for them and more because he figured it may never happen? In many ways, Nate lived in the here and now. He never lost sleep over what the next day would bring, and for the most part he didn't dwell on the past.

"Don't get mad when I say this, but I don't think he's trying to control your relationship. I think he was just being a typical guy. And unfortunately, they don't always use their brains."

"You and Sara might be right. Still, I need to sort stuff out." Lauren took another sip of her milk. "How do you survive with four brothers, anyway? Are they all younger?" Over the past few years she'd met many of Callie's cousins, but with the Sherbrookes being such a large family it was difficult to remember all the specific relationships.

"Trent and Grayson are older. Derek is my twin, and Alec is two years younger."

She remembered meeting Trent and Alec, the other two didn't sound familiar.

"What's it like with that many brothers?"

While Lauren finished her milk, Allison kept her entertained with stories about her brothers. From the sound of it, her relationship with them wasn't much different than any other brother-sister relationship, despite the family's wealth.

"Your brother Trent sounds a lot like my brother. He always thinks he's right, too. Must be an older brother syndrome or something."

"Must be. Sara's complained about the same thing, too." Allison looked across at Lauren, and her carefree smile faded away. "I think I'm ready for bed now. But, Lauren, whatever you decide about your engagement, don't rush your decision. Take your time and think it through. And if you want to talk again, I'll be here all weekend. I know you'd probably rather talk to Callie, but if you need a fresh pair of ears, I'm around, too."

Prior to this weekend, Lauren had only interacted with Allison a handful of times, and she appreciated the other woman's kind gesture. It never hurt to bounce ideas and thoughts off more than one person.

"Thanks. I might take you up on that. See you in the morning."

Alone once again, Lauren stared down at the empty mug, just as awake now as she had been when she came downstairs. Still, her trip to the kitchen had not been a total waste. Allison had given her a lot to think about. Her opinion not only made her think, it gave her hope. If Nate omitted the information about a possible move because he thought it might never happen rather than because he wanted complete control of their relationship, it put a different spin on things. How was she to know for sure, though?

"Sitting in here isn't going to help." She came to her feet. Even if she didn't fall asleep, her bedroom upstairs would be a more comfortable place to contemplate her future.

Chapter 15

"You did what?" Callie asked in a voice so loud Lauren suspected everyone in Cliff House heard her.

"Callie, you heard me. I gave Nate back the engagement ring."

Callie leaned forward, her eyes fixed on Lauren's. "Have you lost your mind? Why did you do that? This doesn't have anything to do with Kevin, does it?"

Unable to hold her friend's stare, Lauren looked away. "Thursday night he dropped this bomb on me. The FBI has this thing called the Hostage Rescue Team. I have no clue what they do, but Nate wants to be a part of it." For the first time since she'd heard the words, she realized she honestly had no clue what the team did. The name implied they rescued hostages, but really they must do more than that. After all, how many hostage situations could there be in the US on a yearly basis?

"Anyway, this week he learned that HRT tryouts start next month. He needs to be down there for the 15th. If he makes the team, he'll need to relocate to Virginia."

Leaning back, Callie's eyebrows creased with confusion. "I understand all that, but I don't see why you called off the engagement. Either push-up or postpone the wedding. Don't call the whole thing off."

"Don't you think he should have told me his plans before now?" she asked, her voice laced with sarcasm. "I feel like he's making all the decisions for us. Controlling our relationship."

"He should have said something sooner, but I don't think he did it because he wants to control you. Think about it for a minute. In all the years you were together, did he ever try to control you? If that was the kind of a guy he was, don't you think he would've done it back then?"

Callie's question cut off any argument she had prepared. She had not stopped to consider that before, but now that she did, Callie was right.

"If you push him away now, you might regret it. Besides, moving isn't the end of the world. I did it. And they need teachers in Virginia, too. Before you do anything, take some time and consider if ending things is what you truly want, Lauren. Maybe go home tomorrow and talk things over with Nate. Explain to him why you got so upset and ask him point blank why he never told you. Then if you decide you still want to marry him, set a new date for the wedding. It would be tight but I think we could get everything rearranged for Fourth of July weekend."

Lauren appreciated Callie's complete honesty. Not that she expected any less. They had been friends too long not to be completely honest and open with each other. She'd done the same thing in the early stages of Callie's relationship with Dylan when they hit a snag.

"Do you think so? I'm not saying I've made my decision, but do you really think we could make it happen for that weekend?"

Callie nodded and squeezed her hand, a small knowing smile on her face. "Just say the word, and I'll make it happen for you guys."

Lauren didn't know what she'd done to get a friend as loyal and loving as Callie, but she was darn glad she had. "As soon as I decide, I will let you know. Now, we probably should get ready for tonight."

***

Kevin surveyed the room. So far that night, he'd been unable to find Lauren, but his instincts told him she was there somewhere. The fundraiser was for a new education initiative that Callie had backed the year before so it made sense that Callie would've invited Lauren, her best friend and fellow educator. They had not spoken since she had returned the ring and he had lost his temper. He'd expected her to come around by now, to realize what she'd given up by turning down his proposal. Yet she hadn't made any effort to contact him. Rather than track her down at her house, he'd decided to purchase a ticket to the fundraiser with the expectation of running into her. Perhaps surrounded by the lifestyle that was within her reach if she married him, she'd reconsider, realizing the mistake she'd made.

He still believed she would eventually regret her decision, but he needed that to happen sooner rather than later. Sherbrooke Enterprises would be calling for bids on their new development soon, and he needed to start positioning himself for the election in another year.

Not to mention, he found himself missing her. That wasn't to say he was heartbroken, but he missed the time they spent together. While she may not be a part of his society, Lauren was a good woman and she'd never made any demands on him. Unlike many of the women he'd dated in the past who were after him for something, she'd never asked for anything but his time.

Finally after thirty minutes of discreetly searching the ballroom, Kevin spotted her in conversation with Allison Sherbrooke. Dressed in the gown she wore to his parents' dinner party, she looked beautiful. An uncommon case of nerves passed through him. Most of the time, he walked into a situation confident he'd get the outcome he wanted, but not tonight. Lauren had already proved she was a wild card in his well-ordered life. Deciding it was better to wait until

Lauren was alone, he snagged an hors d'oeuvre off the tray of a passing waiter, all the while keeping Lauren in his sight.

At least I look like I belong. Lauren surveyed the other guests mingling in the ballroom. She'd picked the Dolce & Gabbana gown Callie gave her for her birthday for the fundraiser. In fact, she'd seen two other women here wearing dresses by the same designer. Shifting her weight to the other foot, she searched for a familiar face among the sea of beautiful well-dressed people. Already she felt out of place, but by standing alone the feeling only intensified. She'd attended several similar fundraisers as Callie's guest in the past. She'd met Kevin at the last one. Tonight, however, she felt more uncomfortable than she had in a while. Kevin's words the night she returned his ring sat in the forefront of her mind. She did only get invited to events like these because of her friendship with Callie. Before he'd said it, she hadn't considered it. Now as she looked around, the truth sank in.

"I thought I'd see you here tonight."

Lauren turned toward the familiar voice. Anyone who could afford a ticket was welcome; still the sight of Kevin surprised her. He'd never struck her as much of a philanthropist. He'd only been at the last fundraiser because his mom wanted someone to accompany her and his father had been sick. "How are you?" Lauren smiled.

"Good, but busy. I spent last week in New Jersey. What about you? Are you here alone tonight?"

"Yes. I got here yesterday. Sara wanted help with some plans for a party."

Kevin's arm brushed against hers when he moved closer. "I've been thinking a lot about you. I miss you, Lauren. Let's start over. Have dinner with me this week." He brushed a hand down her neck, and Lauren took a step back before she realized she'd done it.

"We can make things work between us." He closed the new gap between them. "My offer still stands." His voice turned seductive. "We make sense together."

Lauren studied Kevin and then looked around the ballroom again. Despite her previous rejection, Kevin wanted her back. Yet even though Kevin offered her a place in the society around her, a chance to no longer just be the tag-along, but to belong, she didn't want it. At the beginning of their relationship, perhaps she had, but what she truly wanted was love. If that meant she never attended another event like this, that was fine.

"I'm sorry, Kevin, but nothing has changed. The kind of marriage you want doesn't work for me."

Kevin's nostrils flared, and the muscle in his jaw flexed. "You won't get another chance, Lauren. Once I leave tonight, I won't be back. "

How had she missed his conceit before? Had he done a better job of hiding it or had she intentionally overlooked it? Either way, it didn't matter. Unlike Nate, Kevin never really knew her. "I know, Kevin. If you'll excuse me, I need some fresh air. It was good to see you again. Enjoy the evening."

Lauren stepped around Kevin without a backward

glance, as snippets from each conversation she'd had that weekend played over in her head. She had allowed the pain from the past to cloud her judgment. She realized that now.

Making her way through the crowd, she spotted Charlie and Jake dancing. With their arms around each other, they moved as one, oblivious to the crowd around them. At a cocktail table along the perimeter, Sara and Christopher sat so close together she was practically in his lap, while their hands were clasped together on the table. Across from them, Dylan sat with an arm around Callie's shoulders.

A knot of pain started in the center of her chest and radiated outward as she watched the other couples. She wanted what they all had and not just with anyone. The same love reflected in these couples burned inside her for Nate. No matter what else happened, he'd always be the one. A move to Virginia was a small sacrifice when she considered the alternative.

***

Two hours after leaving Cliff House Sunday morning, with a promise to call Callie and let her know how things went, Lauren pulled into the driveway at Nate's apartment. She was halfway up the steps near the garage when Mrs. Callahan came out of her house.

"Lauren, what you doing here?" She stopped at the bottom of the steps.

Her reason for being there seemed obvious. "I'm

here to see Nate."

"Why would he be here, dear? Isn't he living with you now?"

Had he moved back into the apartment without telling his mom? Did she not know the engagement was off? Since she planned to rectify her mistake, she decided not to mention it now. Thinking fast, she came up with an excuse to explain her presence. "He mentioned that he might pick up more of his stuff today while I was in Newport. I thought he might still be here. I haven't stopped home yet."

"No, I haven't seen him all weekend. Say hi to him for me when you see him. And maybe one night this week the two of you can come over for a cookout and fill me in on the wedding plans."

Lauren walked back down the stairs and gave the woman a quick hug. "Sounds good. How about Wednesday night?"

"I'll invite Ryan over, too," Mrs. Callahan said, smiling. With plans to have dinner with his parents later in the week decided, Lauren headed for home.

Nate's Mustang was parked in the garage when Lauren pulled in. *Should've known.* Why she thought he wouldn't stick around and try to change her mind was beyond her. After all this time she should know Nate Callahan better than that. Even though he'd gone against her wishes, she didn't mind. It showed how much he loved her and how determined he was to keep her in his life.

Lauren walked into her kitchen and heard the lead character from one of Nate's favorite action movies giving the villain an ultimatum in the living room, but otherwise the house remained silent. Not even Maggie and JoJo came into the kitchen.

"Hello." Silence answered as she dropped her purse and crossed into the living room. In the doorway she paused, taking in the sight before her. Nate was stretched out on the couch, an arm behind his head, looking more delectable than he had any right to. Maggie slept down by his feet, while JoJo had managed to sandwich herself between Nate and the couch cushions. If she came home to a sight like this every day for the next fifty years, she'd be a very happy woman, no matter where they lived.

Leaning down she nudged his shoulder. "Nate." When he didn't respond, she nudged him again and spoke a little louder.

Nate blinked a couple of times. Then his hazel-blue eyes locked on hers. "You're home." He pulled himself up and swung his legs off the couch. "What—"

"I need—" she said at the same time.

"Don't say you need me to leave." Nate got out before she finished her sentence. "That's not happening."

"Nate, I—"

"Don't say it. Hear me out first." He stood and put a hand on each of her shoulders as if to hold her in place. "If you don't want to move, that's fine. I won't try for HRT. You're a hell of a lot more important to me than that. Than anything, in fact. I screwed up once before with you, and I'm not doing it again. If you need me to prove it to you then I will. Just tell me how."

Tears prickled the back of her eyes. He might not use the most flowery words, but what he said went straight to her heart. "Can I talk now?" she asked with a sniffle.

Nate gave her a stiff nod, his mouth set in a frown.

"Thursday night I overreacted. Your news blindsided me. It brought back memories of when you left after high school. All the emotions I felt then shot through me Thursday night. It was like living a nightmare all over again."

Guilt clouded his expression, but he maintained eye contact.

"Now that the shock has worn off, I realize it doesn't matter where we are. And you were right, I have wanted to try living somewhere else, but I have never had any reason to move."She placed her hands on either side of his face."I'm looking forward to moving."

She expected a radiant smile from him. All she got was a slight curve of the lips.

"Are you sure? If I do this, I could be away for long periods of time. There is constant training, and other agents tell me it can be hard on relationships."

He'd turned on the movie to pass the time until Lauren came home. He'd prepared a speech, but as it turned out it wasn't necessary. She'd reached the same conclusion he wanted on her own. Even so, he needed her to fully understand what she was agreeing to. No job was worth risking losing her all over again. All she had to do was say the word and his ass would stay in Boston.

"Please. I can take anything the FBI throws at me." She tossed him a saucy grin, making the dimple in her cheek appear.

He tightened his grip on her shoulders. "I'm serious. Divorce rates are high among HRT agents."

Her grin disappeared. "I'm serious, too. Whatever comes up, we will deal with it. That's what married couples do."

This time he let himself smile. "Make me one promise. If you can't handle it, talk to me. Don't bottle it up until you explode and all hell breaks loose."

"Who? Moi?" She tickled him right below his rib cage.

He trapped her hand under his. "Yeah, you. I want to hear you say it."

"I promise. There will be no hell breaking loose."

The knot of anxiety and dread in his gut melted as joy radiated through him. "Can we swing a wedding before I leave?" Waiting any longer than necessary would be akin to torture.

"How does Fourth of July weekend sound? Callie's already rescheduling things."

No words could do justice to how he felt about this woman who was not only his love, but also his best friend. So rather than even try, he grabbed her by the arm and pulled her toward the bedroom. They made it into the hall before he wrapped his arms around her and dragged her against him. Before he could lower his mouth to hers, Lauren took control. Reaching up, she took possession of his mouth, her breasts crushing against his chest. Fire shot through him at the first pass of her tongue against his. Any thoughts evaporated as his body's desires took over. Driven by the need to see all of her, touch all of her, he reached up and untied the knot behind her neck that held up the top of her sundress. Then he took a step back, and with a slight tug he pulled the dress down. When it hit her ankles, she stepped aside and reached for the button on his shorts.

"Not yet. You're still far too dressed." He pulled at the front of her strapless bra before reaching between her breasts to unhook it. He didn't deserve this gorgeous woman, but she was his, and he'd do anything for her. "Much better, but still not done." He ran a hand down her side to her hip. When her breathing changed and her nipples popped, he smiled. Then he hooked a finger under the waistband of her panties and pulled them down as well. "Perfect."

Lauren shook her head and took a step back when he reached for her again. "I don't think so, Major Callahan." Then she again reached for the button on his shorts. As she worked on them, he pulled his shirt off and added it to the growing pile in the hallway.

"In a rush are you?" she gave him a seductive smile, and he almost lowered them both the floor right there in the hall. She ran a hand down his erection, her hand scorching his skin even through the cotton between them.

When he groaned, she smiled and then finally pulled down the final barrier between them.

"Now, that's—"

Nate kissed her again as he picked her up and joined their bodies fully before they made it through the doorway.

His body sated, he dropped a kiss on her head. In response, she snuggled closer to him and closed her eyes. How had he managed the past fifteen years without her? Just the past few days had been hell. Not that any of it that mattered anymore. The wedding was back on and nothing short of a natural disaster was going to change that. A smile that spread throughout his body took shape on his face. Life didn't get much better than this.

Chapter 16

In just two weeks they got everything done, thanks to Callie and her connections. Even with Callie's help, it had not been easy. Still, here she was dressed in the wedding gown of her dreams. Outside family and close friends waited on the South lawn of Callie and Dylan's estate in Greenwich, Connecticut.

Lauren's fingernails dug into her palms, while behind her the hairstylist secured her veil. Already, the woman had admonished her for fidgeting. She didn't want another scolding. Yet it took all her concentration to keep her legs still. Every inch of her quivered with happy excitement. How could she not? After what felt like a lifetime, she and Nate were going to say their vows to each other. She'd thought about this moment since the day in middle school when she'd opened her locker and found a note from him asking her to the movies. Before that day, they had been the best of friends. After that day everything changed. Back then she never would've imagined all the detours their relationship would take, yet somehow, even then, she'd seen them at this point, committing to spend their lives together.

The hairstylist slipped one last pin into her hair and stepped away, leaving Lauren to admire her reflection in the mirror.

"I'm so happy for you. If anyone deserves this, you two do." Callie walked up alongside her. Dressed in a floor-length lilac gown with a full skirt, no one would ever guess she was pregnant.

"I can't believe we managed to pull it all together. I never could've done it without you." The amount of work Callie put into the preparations overwhelmed her. Every day for the past two weeks the two of them had worked on some aspect of the wedding.

"I still don't know how you two did it," Mallory, Matt's wife and one of her bridesmaids, said from across the room.

Callie waved off the comment in true Callie manner. "Are you still going to look at houses in Virginia next week?"

"We both know that when Nate decides he wants something he doesn't fail. The sooner I start looking, the better. Charlie offered to help me."

The corners of Callie's mouth turned downward. "It's going to stink having you that far away."

Her heart grew heavy with the reminder of her pending move, but the memory of waking up with Nate beside her the morning before sprang up and once again filled her with joy. "Think road trip, chickie."

Lauren turned at the sound of the bedroom door opening behind them. "Everyone is ready," Kelly said, returning from downstairs. Dressed in the same gown as Callie, Kelly looked fantastic. Unless someone knew, no one would ever guess she'd had a baby a few months earlier.

Lauren fought the urge to throw her arms over her head and dance around as if she'd just discovered a winning lottery ticket. She managed to physically control herself but her insides were another story altogether." Let's get this show on the road, ladies." She didn't wait around for a response. Instead, she headed downstairs to the foyer where her father waited.

Large puffy white clouds dotted the otherwise blue sky. Only family and close friends sat on the perfectly aligned white chairs on the flawless green lawn. Next to him stood his best man and older brother, Ryan, along with Scott Daily, a close friend and fellow Marine, and Justin Billings.

"It's about time this happened," Ryan said, his voice low so only Nate heard.

Nate controlled himself. He wanted to burst out in a grin. In fact, since she'd proposed today as a wedding date, he'd been going around smiling like an idiot. More than one person at work complained he looked too happy. Even so, he found it difficult to stop the smile from popping out.

As one, the guests stood when the musicians began the wedding march. Like a scene from a movie, he watched transfixed as Lauren made her way down the aisle with her father. When they reached him, Mr. McDonald shook his hand and said something, though the words didn't register in Nate's brain.

"You look amazing." Nate squeezed the words out around the giant lump in his throat.

Lauren smiled up at him. "You clean up well yourself."

From his spot on the temporary altar, the minister began the ceremony by explaining to all present how sacred marriage was. "Today the bride and groom have prepared their own vows," the minister said, with a nod in Nate's direction.

The words he'd agonized over for the past two weeks appeared in his mind. They'd never go down as the most poetic vows in history, but they came from his heart. "Lauren, we played together as babies. Learned to ride our bikes together when we were kids, and fell in love as teenagers. You're my first and only love. I'll always be right by your side."

Even with the few tears sliding down her cheeks, Lauren looked radiant as he slipped the wedding band on her finger.

"Nathaniel Callahan, I have loved you all my life. You were the first boy I ever kissed, and you will be the last man I ever kiss. Regardless of what else life has in store for us, I know we'll face it side by side." Lauren slid his ring in place. Before she even finished, he tugged her toward him and sealed their vows with a kiss. Immediately, applause and a shout of, "Ooh-rah," from his fellow Marines exploded around them.

As the noise subsided, Nate heard the minister clearing his throat. He'd jumped the gun with the kiss, but he didn't care. This was their wedding, and finally Lauren was his wife. Man, he loved the sound of that. After one final taste of her lips, he pulled back and looked over at the minister, who stood there with his lips pinched and his eyebrows raised behind his glasses.

"Just couldn't wait," Nate said with a shrug.

The minister shook his head and continued on, "By the powers vested in me, I now pronounce you man and wife. *Now* you may kiss the bride."

Nate captured her mouth once again and another round of applause broke out. *Finally,* his entire body screamed.

Lauren pulled back first. "The sooner we get this reception started, the sooner we can be alone," she whispered in his ear.

"I like the way you think, Mrs. Callahan." He gave her one last brief kiss before they started down the aisle together.

THE END

Coming next year
Book 1 in a whole new series by Christina Tetreault
as well as
Book 5 in The Sherbrookes of Newport Series.

23165477R00137

Made in the USA
Charleston, SC
11 October 2013